THE
FOURTH
REALM

J. WAYNE STILLWELL

authorHOUSE®

AuthorHouse™
1663 Liberty Drive
Bloomington, IN 47403
www.authorhouse.com
Phone: 1 (800) 839-8640

Published by AuthorHouse 11/15/2019

ISBN: 978-1-7283-3637-4 (sc)
ISBN: 978-1-7283-3635-0 (hc)
ISBN: 978-1-7283-3636-7 (e)

Print information available on the last page.

Any people depicted in stock imagery provided by Getty Images are models,
and such images are being used for illustrative purposes only.
Certain stock imagery © Getty Images.

This book is printed on acid-free paper.

Because of the dynamic nature of the Internet, any web addresses or links contained in
this book may have changed since publication and may no longer be valid. The views
expressed in this work are solely those of the author and do not necessarily reflect the
views of the publisher, and the publisher hereby disclaims any responsibility for them.

This is a work of fiction. All of the characters, names, incidents, organizations, and dialogue
in this novel are either the products of the author's imagination or are used fictitiously.

DEDICATION

This book is dedicated to the survivors of the 21st century.

DISCLAIMER

This book is a fiction contrived and created from the mind of the author. "The Fourth Realm" is a composite of new and old. The best vignettes from my previous books were leveraged and weaved together where it made sense to create a new story. Any reference to persons living or dead is purely accidental and unintended. Nothing in this book ever happened in the real world.

AUTHOR'S PREFACE

"The Fourth Realm", is a fiction story about intergalactic intrigue, mind-boggling technology and desires for world dominance driven by love, power and hate.

The story begins in the year 2049. Nations were struggling to deal with multiple threats to their way of life. The great American experiment was in serious trouble due to the same social and economic chaos that caused the Great Depressions in 1929 and 2023.

This time however, it was worse. A strange mixture of nationalism and socialism led to complete political gridlock. The failure of nationalism led to socialism. Too many consumers and not enough producers put governments in precarious financial positions. Most countries were using their entire tax revenue to service debt.

The situation was exacerbated by global warming and the great migrations. Hordes of people from Africa and South America were legally and illegally moving to Europe and North America. Countries with predominantly European heritages resented the dilution of their cultures by people of color who they felt were bringing their country with them rather than assimilating. Racially motivated populists were calling for authoritarian nationalists to rise up and take back their countries.

What followed was the darkest period in history for intelligent life in the Orion belt of the Milky Way Galaxy. Brutal dictators came to power on Earth and the Rendinese planet Xylanthia in the Sirius Star System. When the American President, Victor Nash, and the alien dictator, Xentorcon, meet, Earth is faced with a grim choice, death or slavery.

Once again, Survivalism became a respected and serious topic in public and in private. The approaches taken were only limited by one's imagination. They ranged from buried backyard habitats to rented Intercontinental Ballistic Missile silos and everything in between. One group chose a radically different option. They decided to leave Earth.

No matter what the reason, immigrating to a distant planet in 2050 would be the equivalent of immigrating from Europe to America in 1620, a one-way trip for the vast majority of people. Imagine saying goodbye to your parents, knowing you would never see them again.

That was the state of affairs in the 5rd decade of the 21st century. Alien dialog has been translated into North American English.

GLOSSARY OF TERMS

Area 51 – Edwards Air Force base test site 80 miles north of Los Vegas, Nevada.

BAS – Brothers and Sisters (BAS) is an underground resistance organization fighting American President Nash's annexing of Canada. The BAS network eventually spread throughout North America.

Containerized Housing Unit – Referred to as "Chews" by soldiers. They can be heated and airconditioned.

Commander Ed Stump - Ex-Navy pilot and now an

Engineering Duty Officer assigned to the nuclear stock pile stewardship program.

Devonian period – Geological period during the Paleozoic era. It occurred approximately 400 million years ago and was dominated by fish and amphibians.

Don Blankenbuehler - head of NASA propulsion research and development."

Gravity Chair – Similar to a fighter pilot's G-suit, the chairs provide a safe work station for Rendinese crews during high acceleration and super light speed travel.

Incubator Station – Suspended animation module used for extended deep space travel and time travel. They are computerized with medical care and relativistic aging control.

Ging Xentorcon – Rendinese political leader who led a coup over the civilian government on the planet Xylanthia and became a dictator.

John Rochester – Head of NASA spacecraft testing. Author off the book "The Cavern Club".

Lasor Defecator – a commode that processes biological waste by turning it into a powdery substance that is easily ejected into space.

Lieutenant Colonel Jeremiah Astor – In overall command of the Army Corps of Engineers division sent to Canada to establish a Garrison in the town of Thompson, Manitoba and to construct a missile site near Baker Lake in northern Manitoba.

Major Ted Hunt – Officer in charge of the combat unit assigned to Colonel Astor's Missile Site construction division.

Miacon – Head of the Rendinese military who conspired against Xentorcon and became leader of the anti- Xentorcon freedom fighters.

Mary Ann Minor – Canadian woman from Thompson, Manitoba and Colonel Jeremiah Astor's love interest. She was also a member of the BAS.

Neil Jansen - Head of NASA's astronaut program.

Pacification Zone – The Rendinese Dictator Xentorcon divided North America up into large pacification zones over seen by Rendinese troopers. A number of zones contained prison complexes that were similar to the Japanese Internment camps used during WW II.

Proxima b – Earth like planet circling Proxima Centauri, one of the stars in the three-star Alpha Centauri star system. Proxima Centauri is a Red Dwarf, the most common star in the Milky Way. Discovered by Angiada-Escude, professor of Astro Physics, Queen Mary University, London, England. Proxima b is slightly larger than Earth, has temperatures that support liquid water and an Oxygen/Argon atmosphere.

Quiet time – In order to deal with Proxima b's constant daylight, colonist scheduled mandatory rest periods every six hours.

Ramacon - Egocentric but capable leader and principal deputy to Emperor Xentorcon.

Rendinese – Alien race that once lived in a time-space continuum abutting Earth's universe. When they realized their universe was collapsing back into a pre-Big Bang singularity, they began to survey the Milky Way looking for a new homeland. They discovered a number of planets, including Earth. They finally chose a planet in the Sirius Star System and spent 22 Earth years migrating their entire population to a planet an Earth astronomer named Xylanthia.

Rendinese Battle Cruisers – Four hundred-thousand-ton war ships; each cruiser can deploy nine squadrons of all-weather fighter interceptors. They are capable of wormhole travel and long-term deployment in deep space.

Rendinese Interceptor – Primary fighter used by the Rendinese military. Capable of endo/exo atmospheric flight; has a crew of four; powered by chemical engines fueled with high energy liquid jell for endo-atmospheric propulsion and high flow cold fusion ion engines for exo-atmospheric thrust. They were upgraded with Anti-Gravity propulsors in Earth year 2038. Armed with missiles, fusion torpedoes and neutral partial beam cannons. Can carry six troopers.

Rendinese Survey Ship – Lightly armed vessel used for exploration. Maximum crew is twelve. They are capable of super light speed and time travel.

Reich – German word for realm or kingdom.

Sally Preston – President Nash's administrative assistant and a covert member of the BAS.

SETI Institute – Worldwide organization committed to making contact with intelligent alien life. They built a phased array antenna complex in Hat Creek, California, 290 miles northeast of San Francisco.

Space Distort Signal Probe – Sensor capable of super light speed and wormhole travel. It is the way the Rendinese communicate long distances and clear space for supper light speed runs.

Ted Jackson - Head of NASA Facilities.

Victor Nash – American politician and right-wing nationalist who won the presidency by promising to purge the government of socialist and return the country to greatness. He was declared President for life by a congress dominated by radical conservatives.

Xylanthia – Planet in the Sirius star system the Rendinese people settled just before their universe collapsed into a singularity. It is in synchronous orbit between Sirius and a companion dwarf star resulting in permeant daylight for half of the planet.

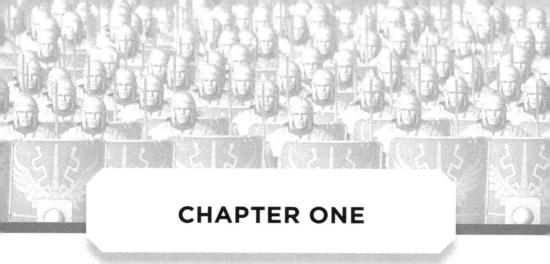

CHAPTER ONE

Birth of a Vision
Place: Shenandoah Valley, Virginia

JOHN ROCHESTER STEPPED ONTO the back deck of his country home to enjoy the sunrise and a cup of English tea. It was November 23, 2049 and his birthday. His children would be arriving in the afternoon to celebrate his birthday and Thanksgiving. He thought about how fortunate he was. He and his wife, Grace, were in their early fifties and in good health. Family wise, life was good.

As he sipped his tea, the glow from the pre-dawn sun provided just enough light for him to see the entrance to the cavern his grandfather Sean and others had constructed to survive the severe 2023 depression. Sealed off with dirt and indigenous landscaping, it was now hidden like an Egyptian tomb, to be discovered by some future explorer.

Memories of the year he spent in the cavern rushed through his head. He remembered the musty smell of the dank animal cave he and his boys were exploring when they discovered the cavern. The drip-drip of water from stalagmites, whispering flutter of bat wings and the trickling sound from a stream serenaded the inhabitants at night.

He remembered the euphoric feeling after kissing Grace for the first time and the disbelief when they discovered the alien space ship in a chamber adjacent the cavern. Where did the time go? We all bonded together during that year. It's amazing, the 'Cavern Club' still exchanges Christmas cards, he thought.

He wondered if he might have to open the cavern up for another stay. Every day the news was worse. Interest rates and unemployment were double digit and rising, the national debt was predicted to reach forty-five trillion dollars. China and other nations were threatening to stop buying U.S. Treasuries.

Countries with national debt equal to 90% or more of their annual revenue were being denied credit from the World Bank. The United Nations was discussing the ramifications of canceling national debts all together. People were coming to the obvious conclusion that the debt would not, nor could it, ever be repaid. Government employees, military and civilian, were threatening to abandon their jobs. He took a sip of tea and went back inside the house. Grace was making coffee.

"Morning sunshine, did you sleep well?"

"In spurts, I can't seem to shut my brain off at night. I worry about the kids, the economy, money and my dreams are crazy," Grace lamented.

"The doctor gave you a pill to take at bed time. Doesn't that help?"

"I don't use them; you know I hate using medicine as a crutch."

"Well, God made whiskey for a reason," he said with a smile as he patted her on the butt.

"Very funny."

"I'm also worried about the future, sweetie. In many ways, it is now worse than it was during the 2023 depression. Some of the people at work are brain storming ideas, but you know, the old cavern is still there."

"Yes, I think about it. The thought of a repeat stay doesn't thrill me."

"We'll see, I need to run into town to gas up the Van and pick up some beer and soda for the weekend. You need anything?"

"A six-pack of canned sleep would be nice."

"We already have that, it's called whisky."

"Funny man, get going, so you can get back."

As he was driving to town, he pondered his life and the current state of affairs. Inspired by his experiences with the Cavern Club and the Rendinese aliens in 2023, he decided to attend the engineering program at Purdue University and then a Masters in Aerospace Engineering at MIT. He applied for the astronaut program as a mission specialist but didn't make the final cut.

The next best thing was a job at the Ames Research Facility located at Moffatt Federal Airfield, in Mountain View, California. Ames is best known for its design of Lunar Atmosphere and Dust Explorer space craft and wind tunnel testing.

In 2031, he was offered a promotion and a transfer to Cape Kennedy, Florida. In 2047, he was offered a job at NASA Headquarters in Washington, D.C. He and Grace were delighted. They bought a home in Leesburg, Virginia which made for a decent commute to work and easy access to the Shenandoah Property his Dad had left him.

Then, the government and civil society started to fall completely apart. Two years after he started his Washington, D.C. job, NASA was declared non-essential and defunded. By 2049, NASA was virtually shut down. Congress had not appropriated funding for the current physical year. Field Centers Like Cape Kennedy. Langley, Ames, Goddard and the Jet Propulsion Laboratory were moth balled. Headquarters was still open but only essential personnel were being paid.

He had worried for some time that he would be declared non-essential. He and Grace had always been frugal and saved 10% of each month's pay. Grace had also inherited some money from her father, but with double digit inflation and loss of income, they knew they would not be solvent for very long.

Place: NASA Headquarters, Washington, DC

His birthday and Thanksgiving a success and the kids gone, he and Grace shut down the Shenandoah house and went home to Leesburg, Virginia. They spent Sunday night watching an old movie and went to bed early. The next day he left for work at 6:00 AM determined to figure out a way forward in an increasingly dangerous world.

At 7:25 AM he walked into NASA Headquarters, sat down at his desk and turned on his computer. As he was clearing E-mail, a Senior Executive Service department head approached him.

"Good morning John" he said.

"Ted, you're in a good mood this morning."

"I'm okay, might as well act like the glass is half full, not half empty. My wife and I decided to stop worrying about things we have no control over. Like death, taxes and the weather."

"And the economic depression and collapse of civil society," John added.

"Well, yes, but not completely. By the way, you free for lunch?"

"Sure, the internet just went down and I don't have any real work to do, so I think I can squeeze in lunch," he replied with a chuckle.

"Meet us at the Big Horn Steak House at 11:30."

"I'll be there."

The Steak House was near the Navy Memorial and the weather was good, so he decided to walk. He arrived at 11:35 AM. Ted, and most of NASA's senior management were already there.

"John, I think you know these guys, but why don't we go around the table anyhow."

"I'm Ted Jackson, Head of NASA Facilities."

"Commander Ed Stump, ex-Navy pilot and now an Engineering Duty Officer assigned to the stock pile stewardship program."

"Don Blankenbuehler, head of NASA propulsion research and development."

"Neil Jansen, head of NASA's astronaut program."

"John Rochester, head of spacecraft testing."

"Great, John, we invited you into the group for several reasons. First, you're in charge of space craft testing, a position that could be most helpful to us. Second, we read your book, 'The Cavern Club'. You have firsthand knowledge about what it takes to survive isolated from normal society. Third, if what you said in your book is true, you have operational knowledge about how a viable space ship would work."

"I understand everything you just said, but what exactly are you trying to tell me?"

"John, just hear us out. We know, and I think you would agree, that things are much more serious than during the 2023 collapse. In 2023, your family chose a survival habitat in a cavern. Some of us went to Canada, others camped in the mountains in an RV. This time we're going to leave Earth and start a new society on either Mars or a Planet in the Alpha Centauri Star cluster."

"What, if by some combination of multiple miracles, we get to Centauri and there is no planet," John asked.

"Valid question but give us some credit for due diligence. I ask a buddy at NASA some time ago about planets in the Centauri cluster. I told him I was helping my son with a school science project."

"And," John said.

"There is an Earth like planet circling Proxima Centauri, one of the stars in the three-star Alpha Centauri star system. Its orbit is in what NASA calls the habitable zone. Proxima Centauri is a Red Dwarf, the most common star in the Milky Way. Proxima b is slightly larger than Earth, has temperatures that support liquid water and an Oxygen/Argon atmosphere."

"Isn't Argon bad for you?"

"Not at all, don't you ever watch Star Trek. Most of the alien planets have oxygen/Argon atmospheres."

"I assume that was a joke. It's okay because Star Trek says so, give me a break."

"No, Teds right. We have studied Oxygen/Argon atmospheres and we would be able to breath normally there," Neil Jansen said.

"Something came up when I was talking with my family. What if the planet is already populated? They might resent us. We'd be like the South America immigrants illegally coming to Europe and America," John cautioned.

"Hopefully, if there is intelligent life on Proxima b, they will be sympathetic to our plight. It will be worth the risk as long as we don't run into what we are running from, I.e. violence, poverty, gangs and tribalism. Hopefully, the Rendinese people you talked about in your book will help us," Ted replied.

"You're asking me to betray the government of the United States?"

"I'm asking you to help us survive the government of the United States."

John looked at Ted and the others, who were staring at John waiting for his reply.

"Well, living in a Cavern would be less risky. I'm still skeptical," John said with a sigh.

"When you've heard it all, you'll be hooked," Ted said.

"I guess so, ha, we can rename Proxima b 'New America'."

"John. That's a great idea. Unless there's an objection, so be it. There remains only one hitch."

"What's that?"

"We don't have a ship."

"And I'm the only one with actual experience flying an interstellar space ship. I see why I'm here. Keep talking," John said.

"For a couple of years, we talked about a habitat somewhere on Earth, you know, just in case. Then when Virgin Atlantic and Space X merged into a global space transportation company called Virgin Atlantic Space, our thinking changed. Their newest space planes were capable of making trips to the moon and back. That made Mars a possibility. Then, when Don Blankenbuehler told us about NASA's new prototype constant thrust plasma ion engine, our discussion changed again."

"Ion engines have been around for years, they don't have the ump to be viable deep space propulsors," John said.

"For extreme distances, yes. But within the solar system, they are viable and the continuous thrust provides artificial gravity for the travelers. By the way John, that engine is part of a compartmented top-secret program which some of us are not briefed into, so be careful with the information."

"Your right about the ion engine John, but this new engine is a major breakthrough. It can produce up to 3 G's, which means we could get to Alpha Centauri in about six years."

"If that is what your plan is, I'm out. I'm too old to burn up six years in a space ship. By the time we get there, Grace and I will be in our mid-sixties."

"I know, but the new engine could get us to Mars in a few months. Nasa has developed a method for generating oxygen using Algae. The oxygenation of Earth 2.54 billion years ago was caused by cyanobacteria. Water is available in the polar regions and UV radiation can be blocked with foil and sunscreen lotion."

"I don't like it; Mars is too close. It would only be a matter of time until some nation or consortium showed up and ruined everything. I'd rather take my chances here on Earth," Neil Jansen complained.

"Right, I suspect all of us feel the same, but we needed to have this conversation. We need all options addressed so we end up on the same page. Now for the real conversation. John, do you remember the Rendinese pilot named Terta?"

"Yes, he was killed in an accident somewhere near Yucca Flats, Nevada. Did you know him?"

"No, but I know about him. He had a son named Terta II. He's in his mid-twenties and still living in Nevada."

"I forgot," John said.

"His mother-in-law and father-in-law are elderly and still alive, but his mother, Bestra, has passed away. Terta-II is the only Rendinese of mating age left as far as we know. Apparently, he is lonely and wants to surrender to Rendinese authorities. My source says he's been communicating with the Rendinese who settled in the Sirius solar system. Sirius is about 8.6 light years from Earth." Ted said.

"How does your source know all this stuff and why would he tell you," John asked with a tone of disbelief in his voice.

"Our source is Terta-II's DOE Psychiatrist, who happens to be Commander Stump's college roommate. His name is Dr. Niski. Ed knew what Niski was doing at Area 51 and after we learned from your book about the capability of Rendinese space craft, we decided that Ed should let his buddy in on our plan."

"How is Terta-II communicating with his people?"

"Apparently, maybe with Niski's help, he has somehow contacted the SETI phased array antenna complex in Hat Creek, California, who agreed to relayed his messages."

"But SETI sights are passive, they only listen."

"Hat Creek has developed a transmission capability for complex modulated signals. They call it METI, Messaging to Extraterrestrial Intelligence system."

"Yes, I guess the Rendinese could pick up the signals with their Deep Space Probes," John added.

"Amazing. The Psychiatrist is probably looking to write a block buster book and the SETI people are living their dream," Ted added.

"So, what's your plan, exactly," John ask.

"We've already agreed that we're going to colonize a planet in the Centauri Star Complex. Hopefully it will be Proxima b."

"I, we, want you and Commander Stump to go to Yucca Flats and make contact with Terta-II.

"You have no idea how difficult it will be to do what you just ask," Stump warned.

"It must be done. Humans will be eating each other soon. If Terta II cannot help us get transport to Centauri, we either stay on Earth or reconsider Mars."

"If this works out, who is going to Centauri," John asked.

"The six of us, our spouses and significant others, direct children and grandchildren. Maybe Dr. Niski. We figure about two dozen people initially."

"A Rendinese survey ship can only accommodate a crew of 12," John warned.

"That's why you're so valuable, John, you know the ship and what has to been done to reconfigure it."

"For such a short trip, we won't need incubation stations. They could be removed. When do I have to commit," John asked?

"As soon as possible, the clock is ticking."

"I'm not promising you anything. Being a 21st century Pilgrim on a one-way trip to infinity makes my heart palpitate. But I'll speak to my family."

"John, you know this has to be considered top secret."

"Of course."

John called Grace and ask her to invite the children, John Jr. and Abby, to come to their Leesburg house at 6:00 PM. He asked her to tell them he wanted to discuss family finances and it was very important. During the drive home his thoughts again focused the cavern Club and Grace. He remembered holding her hand and walking along the edge of the underground stream that flowed along the north side of the cavern.

The stream flowed slowly and made just enough sound to make muffled conversation easy. They knew eyes and ears were probably watching them. He led her to the waterfall feeding the stream and then into a crevasse behind a big stalagmite. At last, some privacy, it was tight, forcing them to press against each other, not suffocating but close enough to feel her breath wash over his face. He gave her a passionate kiss. It was their first.

Grace did not try to move away, she pressed closer, their heart beats racing, bodies reacting, her breasts pressing against his chest. He moved his hands slowly up from her waist to her breasts.

"John, your making me crazy, we need to get back. This is not the place and time."

"Only if you tell me something."

"What?"

"That you'll be my girl."

John had dreamt and re-dreamt those moments for the last eighteen years. He could see her in his mind's eye. She was the most beautiful dish water blond he had ever met. 5' 8" tall and 125 pounds with a bikini body and girl next door looks. He often wondered why she fell in love with a 6', 180 lb. average looking Navy midshipman without a car. All he knew was he was a lucky man. His thoughts were interrupted by breaking news on the radio.

"We interrupt our regular broadcast for breaking news from South Korea. The North Koreans have invaded South Korea. Sole is under siege and expected to fall by the end of the day. Sources in Europe say Russia is staging forces near their border with Kazakhstan and Belarus. The President has announced that we are at DEFCON III."

John turned off the radio. It depressed him. Soon he was home.

"Hi sweetie, how was your day,"

"Nothing special. Went to the gym, did some shopping and then to the grocery store. Supper is TACO Salad. You and the kids love it and it's an easy one course meal."

"Great, I'm going to wash up."

While he was cleaning up and changing into casual clothes, the kids showed up.

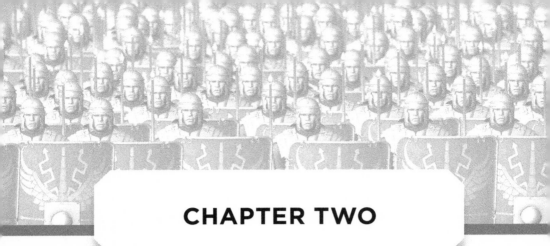

CHAPTER TWO

The commitment

Place: Rochester home, Leesburg, Virginia

JOHN LOOKED AT HIS watch. It was already 7:15 PM. They had eaten supper on the deck because the weather was so nice. His oldest son smoked an occasional cigar and offered one to him. He looked at it.

"What the hell, why not," he said.
"I figured since we're outside, mom would not be upset."
"We just need to make sure we stay down wind of her."

They talked about school issues, politics, Abby's new boyfriend and repairs on the Shenandoah house. Grace mostly listened. She knew at some point the conversation would get very serious.

"Okay Dad, everyone's full of Taco Salad, thanks mom, it was great as always. I just smoked a cigar with my Dad and the weather is beautiful. What's going on with family finances? You either hit the lotto or you're broke."

John laid his cigar in an ash tray, looked at Grace and signaled his intent by starting to clear the table. She got up to help. With the table cleared, John started the conversation.

"I'm sure that everyone's been watching the news. I don't want to be too fatalistic, but we may be watching the beginning of the end," John said.

"Or the end of the beginning. That's from a Churchill speech during WW II," John Jr. said.

"You're right, but it doesn't really matter, the situation remains the same, human society on this planet is in trouble. We have to look at our options."

"This is de ja vu all over again. The Cavern Club was a good answer last time, why can't we just open it up and use it again," Grace asked.

"I, and others, believe this is not the end of the beginning, it is much worse. A social and economic Armageddon is coming where sovereign nations will disintegrate into tribes. A dangerous mix of a Mad Max movie and North American Indian like culture. Warring tribes with 21st century weapons and tools."

"Wow, that would be scary," John Jr. said.

"We have three options, stay put and hope for the best, open up the Cavern for another stay or a third."

"What's that, Dad," Abby asked.

"Leave the Earth."

"Come on husband. That's absurd. There is no way we can get to a new planet. I know your beloved NASA is good, but they have nothing capable of practical interstellar travel. We couldn't live long enough to reach the closest star system. Our grandchildren's descendants might see the new world, but we would die in the lonely vacuum of space. I know you're trying to think out of the box, but no thanks."

"Remember Terta, Atium and Mana."

"The aliens you wrote about in your book."

"Atium and Mana are still alive and living at a DOE facility in Yucca Flats. Terta and Bestra have died, but they had a son they named Terta II. He wants to return to his people. We're going to contact him and ask for a ride to a planet in the Alpha Centauri star complex."

"Cool, we'll be 21st century galactic hitch hikers," Abby joked.

"What if the planet is already populated. They might resent us. We'd be like illegal immigrants," John Jr. said.

"Maybe, but we're going for the same reason all immigrants do, because it sucks where they are living. They want to get away from violence, poverty, gangs and tribalism. We'll be creating a new country where Grace and I can watch our descendants pursue the American dream, or Proxima b dream. We'll call the planet New America," John said.

"I get it, like New England or New Mexico," John Jr. said.

"If Alpha Centauri doesn't work, we can go to Sirius and live with the Rendinese.

"That's a lot to digest," Grace lamented.

"The people I've met with want a commitment soon."

"What people," Grace asked.

"Basically, the leadership of NASA in Washington."

"My god John, the conspiracy of all conspiracies. If you get caught, they'll charge you with treason."

"That why, as a family, we must pledge complete secrecy and unless we all go, no one goes."

"I agree with that," Grace said.

"I'm going to tell the group that I'll have an answer in 48 hours. Can we all agree on that?"

Everyone agreed. That night he didn't get much sleep. John tossed and turned, unable to shut off his mind. He would doze off for ten or fifteen minutes and awaken, roll on to his side, trying not to disturb Grace, and force himself to reenter his dream. Fear immediately intruded on his thoughts. He tried to force himself to think about sex with Grace or lust after a faceless woman. Every time, anxiety pushed its way into the privacy of his sub conscience mind.

He tried to read, checking the time every minute or so, finally dozing off with the book laying on his chest. The light in the room remained on and startled him when he awoke thirty minutes later. It was not dawn; the lights were only a reminder of his fitful sleep. Asleep again, his sub conscience mind lost the battle with fear and he was awoken after seeing his children lost in space with no food and oxygen running out. Grace was being chased by a monster on some distant planet.

It was only 1:20 AM, he was desperate for peaceful sleep, not just for fatigue or his mind, but for escaping the anxiety he felt in his conscious mind that couldn't be dismissed by rationalizations. He saw himself flying over a strange land. He was soaring over an endless grave yard. His entire genealogy lay below him documented on grave stones. When he saw the graves of Grace and their boys, he woke up but didn't open his eyes.

He thought about a tree that falls in a forest and no one was present to hear it. But he could hear it in his head as his minds eye watched it fall. The mind cannot be denied. What the mind sees and hears cannot be managed. He adjusted his pillow. It was nearly 3:30 AM. He is certain he heard foot-steps. Was it one of the boys? No, they are grown but he wished they weren't.

He switched on the ceiling fan, hoping the soft sound of the repetitive wisps made by the large blades as they moved the air would provide white noise sufficient to ease his sleep. Dreams were filled with goodbyes to his extended family and how to do it without compromising their escape. Finally, he heard the rustle of birds fluttering through the large Forsythia next to his bed room window. Grace would be up soon and the lonely twilight zone survived until the next night.

Place: NASA Headquarters

That morning at work, Ted was not happy with John's conditional yes but he accepted it.

"John, we feel the urgency to move forward is ever increasing. Last night one of my accounts was frozen. It's with a small credit union in Indiana where I did my undergraduate work. I didn't have a lot of money there but it's a warning that portends bad things to come. The group has agreed that we need to start moving to cash as fast as possible."

"I understand what you're saying. Bank failures foretell bad things. It will take time to move to cash. My debit and credit cards have daily and cash withdrawal limits."

"We're in the process of increasing the daily withdrawal limits on our debit cards. You and Grace should do the same and don't forget the kids if they have accounts. One more thing, sleeping bags. Here's the ordering information for a military high-performance sleeping bag. It's water and bug proof, vented and safe down to -20 F. They're expensive, but safety of our families is more important.

"Got it. I think I can increase my limits on line. I'll give it a shot."

"Good, otherwise, it's business as usual. We don't want people to become suspicious. We'll talk later."

John finished up a budget package review for the National Nuclear Security Administration's (NNSA) mothball program. During lunch he turned on his lap top and tried to increase the daily withdrawal limits on his cards. In every case he ended up on the phone with a bank representative, but he got it done. On the way home he withdrew $6,500 from ATM's.

Rochester home, Leesburg, Virginia

"Anything exciting happen today," as he gave Grace a quick hug.

"Other than worry, pretty routine. Been talking to the kids. Last night was a significant emotional event for all of us."

"Tell me about it. Ted said one of his banks froze his accounts. I think it's just the beginning, an omen, a warning."

"That's scary, John, I have always worried about being broke again, like when we were first married."

He opened his briefcase and laid $6,500 on the table.

"What's that for?"

"I increased the daily limits on our cards. We need to leave enough on account to pay our mortgage and living expenses, but from now on we should withdrawal $2,000 to $3,000 every week, mostly from savings."

"What do we do with all that cash?"

"Nothing for now, this is a defensive financial move. If by some miracle the world regains its sanity, we'll put it back in the bank."

"What did the kids have to say about last night?"

"It was mixed, as you would expect. It was also revealing."

"How so?"

"Abby told me that two weeks ago, she was accosted in the Greenland Mall parking lot by a group of boys."

"What! They didn't..."

"No, no, she wasn't hurt in any way. They were looking for money but it scared the hell out of her."

"Another omen."

"We also talked about people in general. For instance, I thought I knew our next-door neighbors. Shelly and I went shopping at the mall. She shoplifted ear rings and a pair of shoes. She put the shoe's on in the store and just walked out. Everybody seems scared and desperate."

"What did Jr. have to say?"

"He's on the fence about all of this. You know your son, if your demand it, he'll comply. His respect for his father is unbounded. He did say he was worried about the company he works for. Their revenues are way down."

"You know where this is heading Sweetie?"

"I know."

"I'm going to fix a drink and call the kids."

"Put them on speaker phone so I can participate."

"Of course."

Five minutes later, John called his son.

"Hello."

"It's Dad, you're on speaker phone."

"Hi son," Grace said.

"Hi Mom, love you."

"love you too Mom."

"Son, this is about our conversation last night. We must make a decision. Banks are starting to fail; people are stealing and becoming dangerous. Did you know your sister was accosted a few weeks ago at the Mall?"

"No, she didn't say anything to me."

"I'm guessing as soon as DOE finishes the mothball plans for their field sites, I will be declared non-essential personnel. Mom said your company is failing and the news media is predicting a shutdown of commerce and return to the barter system. I think we need to commit to the Yucca Flats option."

"I've talked with Patty. She's for it if you think it's the best way."

"I think it's the best way. Start accumulating some cash, whatever you can afford and I'll get back to you on the rest of our plan. We can always back out later if we don't like how things are going."

"Agreed."

"Okay son, I'm going to call your sister now. Love you."

"Love you too Dad."

"Hopefully Abby will be home."

"Hello."

"Hi Abby. You're on speaker phone."

"Hi Abby, love you," Grace said.

"Love you too Mom. This must be bad news; you never call me during the work day."

"Not bad news pe se, but serious news. Mom and I just talked with Jr. and agreed that we need to commit to the Yucca Flats option we talked about last night. Things are going to hell my daughter. The agreement is to commit today with the option down the road that any of us can drop out if things aren't going well."

"Okay, Dad, I trust you."

"This won't happen immediately. Start drawing some cash from your bank, just what you can afford and I'll get back to you on other preparations."

"Okay, love you."

"Love you too."

John embraced Grace. I sure hope I know what the hell I'm doing."

"You always have my love."

"Thanks. Unless I learn something different, each of us should put one suitcase together. Fill it with simple cloths, like jeans and slip on tops; basic toiletries, a few pictures, birth and wedding certificates, a 90-day supply of medicines, cash and non-perishable snacks, like jerky and energy bars.

Everyone should wear a coat and a new pair of durable shoes. I'll be ordering enough high-performance sleeping bags for everyone. Be prepared to leave on a moment's notice, which could be in a few weeks."

"I think I've got the picture."

"I'll share with you any specific plans the group has tomorrow night. We can also tell the kids about the preparation they need to make for departure."

"Wow, I feel like I'm in a science fiction movie."

"Maybe we are," John joked.

He and Grace went to bed at 10:00 PM. In REM, he found himself falling from nowhere to nowhere. He was back in the twilight zone enduring the inevitable gauntlet of anxiety driven fears about the future.

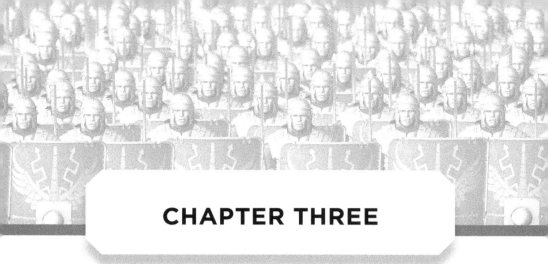

CHAPTER THREE

Rendezvous in the desert
Place: Washington, D.C.

TRAVELING BETWEEN LEESBURG AND Washington, D.C. is an east/west commute that guarantees the sun will be in your face the entire trip. John often told Grace that if he had it to do over again, he would've bought a house south of Washington. This particular morning, the sun seemed brighter than ever. Everyone was driving with their sun visors down and squinting which slowed the traffic to half the speed limit.

To help with boredom, he changed his radio from music to NPR. There was breaking news about the state of the country and President Nash. He'd been in the news frequently since black Wednesday, the day the Dow Jones Average lost 900 points. Victor Nash was a radical populist and right-wing nationalist with plans to purge socialist and liberals from the government and return power to the states.

NPR's reporting was alarming. Congress was considering allowing Nash to serve a third term or possibly be declared President for the duration of the crisis. The president was quoted as saying that he needed the extra time to reshape the country.

"The man wants to be dictator. God help us," he thought.

After a two-hour commute, he was already worn out and hadn't reached his desk yet. During the morning he worked on budget items, a presentation for the Directors Monday morning staff meeting and cleared E-mail on the internet and the firewalled DOE intranet. At lunch, the Yucca Flats group, as John called them, had lunch at a local restaurant.

"I've got some news, but first we need to hear from John," Ted said.

"I figured I was on your minds. The answer is yes, I'm in. But I reserve the right to back out if all this blows up in our faces."

"Fair enough. Commander, tell everyone what you told me this morning."

"Just a minute, I've been watching the man sitting two tables from us. He keeps looking our way. I think he's trying to listen to our conversation. I don't think we should talk in a public place anymore," Ted whispered.

"Then let's leave. I'll leave a tip for the waitress."

On the way back to Headquarters, they picked up sandwiches at a deli and reconvened in a conference room.

"Okay Commander, I think you can continue now."

"I went over to Andrews Air Force base after work last evening. I'm not currently qualified, but I used to be a Navy pilot. I put my wings on and spoke with the officer on duty at air operations. They're under a tight budget like everybody else, but the wings got me consideration that others might not get. I told him I needed a

Military Airlift Command flight, what we call a MAC flight, to Nevada and I would have a NASA SES-III with me. That helped also, because SES-IIIs gets the same treatment as flag officers."

"Did you get a ride?"

"Yes, day after tomorrow, 12:45 PM departure. It's a non-stop to Nellis AFB, which is about 10 miles north of Las Vegas. We'll rent a car and drive to Nye, Nevada. The Bren Tower, constructed to check out nuclear bomb fusing is there and it's now a tourist site. It's close to the Yucca Flats DOE controlled house complex where Terta II and his in-laws live."

"Will Terta II know we're coming?"

"Yes, I'll let Niski know."

"Are you sure we can trust the doctor," John asked.

"Pretty sure, he's been smuggling Terta II's communiques out to the SETI people. He's already up to his neck in this."

"I assume the objective is to ask for Terta II's help getting us to Centauri. What's in it for him?"

"We will smuggle him and his in-laws out of Yucca Flats to a remote camp site in the Desert National Wildlife Refuge, northeast of Vegas. The rest of our group will be waiting there. The quid pro quo is Terta-II and his family will be reunited with his people covertly without triggering a military response. He knows the last time that happened, the Rendinese won but many also died.

Niski heard that the security people have been told, quote, 'to kill the alien captives if Rendinese warships try to free them.'"

"The only reason they would let Terta II know that is if they knew he was communicating with his people. I don't believe they would actually do it, Earth would gain nothing," John surmised.

"If it's true, our job is to make sure their extraction is totally covert.

"Okay, but this is going to be tuff. When do you want to leave for Andrews," John asked?

"We'll leave from work at 9:00 AM on Thursday," Commander Stump said.

That night, John briefed his family about his trip and the preparations they needed to make. He guessed he'd be away for a week. Thursday came fast and by 1:00 PM they were in the air.

Place: Beatty, Nevada

"I just got a text from Niski. He said he'll meet us at Gema's Wagon Wheel Restaurant in Beatty at 6:00 PM."

"Where's that," John ask.

"GPS says about 8 miles from Yucca Flats and the internet says it's a small town of about a thousand people."

"Okay, I'm going to try and catch a nap."

By 5:20 PM Ed and John were parked in the Wagon Wheel Café parking lot. At 5:55 PM a man rapped on their car window. It was Niski.

"You Commander Stump," he asked.

"Yes, this is John Rochester."

"I figured, you two look like Washington bureaucrats."

"Hey, be nice. How's Ann?"

"She's fine Ed, nice to see you again. Let's go inside and have a cup of coffee."

They chose a corner booth and sat down. An attractive waitress approached the table and wiped it off with a wash cloth. The top button of her blouse was undone, an age-old trick that helps increase tips. The three of them quietly enjoyed the view. She knew they were looking.

"Our special today is Chicken fried steak with mash potatoes and carrots. What would you like to drink?"

"That sounds good and three coffees."

After the waitress served them, Niski began the conversation.

"I'm going to cut to the chase. I need both of you here in six weeks. That would be Thursday, May 16th with $10,000 in cash."

"What's the money for?"

"To pay from ambulance driver credentials and the loan of an ambulance. We'll met at Johnson's Ambulance service on the main drag in Beatty. You two are going to drive to Yucca Flats, pick up Terta II and his in-laws. Your story, if anyone ask, is you're taking them to Nellis Air Force Base for an annual physical and CT scans. I'll grease the skids and follow you."

"So, how many more people have you told about us?"

"No one, Johnson didn't ask and he doesn't care. He's got a gambling problem and is in serious trouble with people in Vegas. All he cares about is the $10,000."

"Where are we actually going?"

"As we have already agreed, to a remote camp site in the Desert National Wildlife Refuge. It's your job to coordinate with the rest of your group. I recommend you have them rent class A motor homes and drive 24 hours a day. They can be at the refuge in a couple of days," Niski said.

Everyone prepared for the trek to Nevada. The head count was 27 men, woman and children. Five class A motorhomes were rented, suitcases packed, bank accounts drained and pets given to good homes or, as a last resort, dropped off at the SPCA. Irreplaceable family documents, expensive jewelry, clothes, and for many, as a grasp at hope, packages of seeds, were all placed in the suitcases.

May 16 was the date, so to allow some cushion, they departed for Nevada on May 12. That would give Ed and John time to meet Niski in Beatty. Everyone was nervous but at dawn on May 12, the caravan departed with the expectation they would never return.

There was an eerie calm aboard the motorhomes as they left Leesburg. People sat quietly watching the world they were so familiar with, and mostly took for granted, pass by. The high school three generations of Rochester's attended. The gym Grace used every day.

The dealership where John had purchased three cars.

"God, I hope we know what we're doing," John thought.

"Dad, what do you think is the best route?"

"I'm thinking the southern route, I-81 south and then I-40 west. There should be less congestion that way."

"Okay, sounds good. I'm going to lay down. When you want relieved, let me know."

"Will do."

The trip progressed without incident. At exits and rest stops there were 'Victor Nash, President for life' signs.

"What do you guys think about Nash being President for life?"

"I don't like it. Too much power for too long. He'll end up being worse than what we have now," Grace answered.

"The medicine might be hard to swallow, but it's going to take a strong leader to fix the mess we're in," John Jr. said.

"Well, we're leaving, right. So, it doesn't matter," Abby lamented.

Many filling stations were out of gas and homeless people were abundant. At every exit, people were trying to hitch a ride somewhere or looking for a handout. They were all glad for the large gas tanks on the RVs. They also brought along the plastic gas cans used to fuel their lawnmowers. They managed to buy enough gas at large truck stops to get them through.

After almost 52 hours on the road, they reached the wildlife refuge and set up camp at the GPS position provided by Niski. John and Ed left for Beatty right away using the subcompact car they towed behind one of the RVs.

In Beatty, they found Johnson's Ambulance Service and pulled in to the parking lot. Niski was waiting outside. Inside they went into a back room and had their photos taken. fifteen minutes later they left with two IDs, two white smocks and one ambulance.

"Follow me and have your IDs ready at the National Test Site entrance."

Place: DOE National Test Site, Yucca Flats, Nevada

Niski had his colonel's uniform on and he was well known. John and Ed were amazed at how easy it was to get on the site. He credited Niski for that. Soon they arrived at Terta II's quarters. Inside were nine people, which was a surprise.

"Gentlemen, this is Terta II, his in-laws, Atium and Mana, and Terta II's five siblings."

"You didn't mention there were five additional children?"

"It doesn't change anything."

"No, except that we now have 36 people to deal with."

"Let's get loaded, it'll be crowded with nine people in the ambulance but it is what it is."

"What if the guards search us?"

"They won't. If they do, I'll tranquilize them."

"Where did you get that," Ed ask.

27

"I'm a colonel and a doctor, I can acquire a lot of things you can't."

As it turned out, passing through the gate was a white-knuckle event but they were not searched.

"Did you notice that one of Terta II's brothers looked different," John ask.

"I didn't look to hard at them. What are you thinking?"

"The young man looks like he's part human. A quick glance from twenty feet away, you would think he is human."

"His name is Tacon. No matter, we have bigger fish to fry," Niski said.

John had spent time with the Rendinese. They all have the same familiar characteristics. Humanoid in general except for their heads, a light chocolate complexion, square face, small nose, piercing yellow/green eyes, a normal mouth and no facial hair. The hair on their heads is always long and pulled back into a pony tail.

Tacon had a small but protruding nose, lighter mulatto skin color and eyebrows. Nothing more was said until they reached the wildlife refuge camp site.

Place: Desert National Wildlife Refuge, Nevada

"Now that we have introduced ourselves to each other, we need to contact SETI and get a message to the Rendinese. Ted, did you guys bring the short-wave radio I ask for?"

"Yes, it's in the first RV."

"Erect the antenna on top of the RV and we'll see if we raise my contact in Hat Creek."

"Terta II, I knew your father back in 2023," John said, trying to break the ice.

"I was a toddler then."

"Of course, my name is John."

"Glad to meet you and thanks for helping my family."

"Your welcome. I don't mean to pry, but I noticed one of your brothers looks different."

"His name is Tacon. My mother had six children. My father was Terta, my younger brother and sisters were inseminated with my Father-in-law's sperm and Tacon had a human father, she called him Paul."

"I knew Paul. Well that explains it. Thanks for sharing."

Later, Abby was collecting firewood and noticed that Tacon was doing the same. She had not really looked at him until that moment but felt a strange affinity toward him. He was different but intriguing. She approached him.

"My name is Abby, what's yours?"

"Tacon, are you in your fertility cycle?"

"What!"

She looked at him with a scowl and then walked away.

He followed and ask her to stop.

"I obviously said something you didn't like."

"Normally, men aren't so crude when talking to a woman they just met."

"For Rendinese, it is a standard exchange. How can I know unless I ask you?"

"You have no need to know and shouldn't ask such questions."

"Rendinese males need to know if the female they are going to make love with is, or is not, in her fertility cycle. If she is and doesn't want to get pregnant, they will wait. It is a show of respect."

"That may be interesting to you but why are you discussing these things with me?"

"I don't understand, I desire to make love with you. It is not normal for the female to refuse."

"If all Rendinese men are as rude as you, it's going to be a long winter."

"What does that mean?"

"Never mind, it's just a saying. I do not wish to speak with you anymore."

With that, Abby walked away leaving Tacon completely confused."

"Hi honey, I saw you talking to Tacon. Is he a nice guy," John ask?

"He has a dirty mind. Two minutes after we met, he wanted to have sex with me. Disgusting."

"Honey, I lived with the Rendinese years ago. They view mating completely different from us. Even after permeant mating, what we call marriage, Rendinese have sex with whoever is willing. I know that makes no sense, but they do it and nobody cares or gets jealous."

"You mean like animals. Freewheeling infidelity, that would never work for me."

"John, we're having a meeting in front of the first RV," Ted yelled.

"Honey, I have to go."

"Dr. Kiski has made contact with Hat Creek and passed on the GPS coordinates of our camp. The Rendinese have replied to Terta

II's message and will be at the camp site mid-afternoon tomorrow. Everyone needs to be ready to go by then."

That night everybody was quiet. They sat watching camp fire flames dance and change color while spewing sparks and whiffs of smoke into the air. The full impact of the 11th hour had landed on everyone. They were actually going to leave Earth, probably forever. Adrenaline rushes, anxiety and difficulty breathing made it hard to stare at the night sky.

Abby caught Tacon staring at her. She rolled onto her side, facing away from him. She wanted to be mad and worried about him sweet talking her into something.

All of a sudden, they heard the sound of a helicopter.

"Everyone stay where they are. It's probably just the park ranger checking on things."

The helicopter got closer and then proceeded to land.

"What the hell," Ted said.

"With the chopper shut down, a woman disembarked and approach everyone, who were all now standing in a group.

"My name is Dr. Nancy Alcome. I'm from Hat Creek. I've been helping Arlene and I'm going with you."

"Just like that, Ted said.

"I've spent my entire life dreaming about contacting aliens. I'm sorry, but I have to do this."

"Ted, I suggest we let her be. If we kick her out, she might, in anger, turn us in or go to the press."

"You're right John, it just aggravates me."

"We should all try to get some sleep. Tomorrow will be a long day.

At 3:15 PM the next day the group was sitting together with their possessions waiting for the arrival of the Rendinese. Most of them did not know what the ship would look or sound like, but they listened and watched anyhow.

"Dad, do you think they will really come," Abby asked.
"Of course, honey," trying to reassure her.

A few minutes later a humming sound could be heard in the distance. It got louder and louder. Nobody was talking. The humming became a low frequency buzz that sounded like a person continuously saying the letter z. A cracking, popping noise, similar to what you would hear from a Van Der Graf generator, randomly modulated the buzzing.

Soon, two massive grey ships, the size of Boeing 747s but with smaller wings and larger fuselages, appeared. They hovered for a minute. The snapping and popping were so loud, people had to cover their ears. Landing legs deployed and the ships settle down onto the desert floor. People started to move toward the ship.

"Everyone stays put, give them time to secure the ship and disembark."

They waited, but not for long. A portal on the starboard side opened up without making a sound. Two Rendinese exited the ship and approached.

"Terta II, you should greet them and assure them that everything is in order," John suggested.

"Welcome to Earth," Terta II said in the Rendinese his mother had taught him.

"Are you ready. Our stealth is good, but we should not delay. If we're discovered, it could lead to bad things," the Rendinese leader cautioned.

Terta II and the leader talked for a moment in Rendinese and then turned to face Ted and John.

"He asked if our papers, DNA, and fingerprints had been taken care of? I assured him that we had scrubbed everything with an acid called Clorox and burned our ID papers, even the RV rental contracts. He's also said that we can board."

They formed a line.

"Why do the ships make so much noise? The one we found in the cavern was much quieter," John said to Terta II.

"I ask the leader the same question. He said the ship has a new, more powerful anti-gravity system that allows them to land and takeoff from planets twice the size of Earth. The old design you are familiar with is much smoother but required the ship to stay clear of high gravity planets."

It took the better part of an hour to board and stow belongings. With everyone in acceleration chairs, an Ark full of 21st century pilgrims left Earth. They prayed that New America would provide what they coveted, life, liberty and the pursuit of happiness.

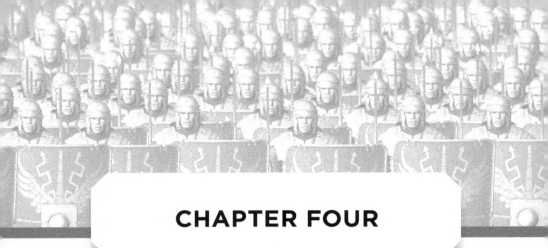

CHAPTER FOUR

New America

Place: Alpha Centauri Star Complex

THE TRIP FROM EARTH to the Centauri Star Complex had not been pleasant. A boring diet, cramped quarters and being stuffed into skin tight acceleration stations tested everyone's metal. They were allowed thirty-minute breaks every two hours to use the laser defecator, eat and stretch their muscles. Thirty minutes was just enough time to identify a safe route for the next super-light speed run.

Several people brought DVDs which were scanned by the ship's computer and feed to the acceleration chair entertainment displays. They watched the movie 'Grease', Ken Burns Civil War documentary and the TV series 'Jessie Stone' over and over again.

The Rendinese knew incubator stations were not necessary for the short trips, so they replaced them with acceleration chairs. That increased the passenger limit to 24. The acceleration chairs were critical. Without them the trip to Centauri would have taken 6 to 7 years because the maximum sustained acceleration humans and Rendinese can stand is about 4 G's. The acceleration chairs allowed the ship to accelerate to super light speed relatively quickly without killing everybody.

Finally, they reached their destination. The New America pilgrims stood looking at Proxima b through the crystal viewing ports of the Rendinese ships they had lived in for the last eight days. Everyone devoured the view before them. They could smell opportunity. They tried to stay out of the way as the crew masterfully prepared for landing.

The Centauri Star Cluster consisted of three stars. Two, Centauri A and B, formed a binary pair while Proxima Centauri, a White Dwarf, was a third of a light year away. Like Earth's moon, Proxima b's rotation is synced with its orbit around the sun. One side in permanent daylight and warm, the other side dark and cold.

They were lucky; young White Dwarfs emit dangerous particles that can erode atmospheres and harm biological life. Proxima Centauri however, was 2 billion years older than Earth's sun and stable.

As the ships entered the atmosphere, it became possible to once again hear the irritating buzzing, popping and cracking the anti-gravity propulsor made as it interacted with Proxima b's gravity. But the view trumped everything. Large greenish-blue oceans, snow-capped mountains and green continents brought out many an awe from the group. Strangely, there were no polar ice caps.

The view from the air was deceiving. The view from the ground was not as appealing, it was primitive with no intelligent life. The land scape was pre-Jurassic, devoid of birds and large mammals. The light radiating from Proxima Centauri as they landed would not reach Earth for over eight years. They had traveled from the 21st century back to the equivalent of Earth's Devonian geological period, almost four-hundred years ago. It was as if the Rendinese ships were time machines.

The ship landed in a clearing and after sensors indicated the atmosphere safe to breath and the temperature a balmy 88 degrees, the hatch opened. The rush of breeze driven air through the cabin was like taking your first shower after walking across a desert. People were told to disembark but to gather by the ship for discussions. Terta II, John and Ted, though unelected, took charge.

"For those of faith, or if your just grateful, please join me in a short prayer," John ask.

Most of the group, except for the Rendinese and a couple of teenagers, kneeled.

"Heavenly father, we are grateful for our safe arrival. Your kingdom is beyond anything most people back home would understand or believe. We ask for a chance to be worthy of everything you have and will bestow upon us. Give us the courage and health to pursue this dream of a new life and look down on us from time to time to make sure were doing okay. We name this planet 'New America" and place it your hands. In Christ name we pray, Amen."

"New America, the new back of the beyond," Commander Stump said.

"The first thing we must establish is a safe way to exist. That means for now, no one is to wonder off alone. We'll move around in groups of three or four. At least one adult in each group will be armed. The use of deadly force however, is a last resort. Any questions," John asked.

"Very well, the Rendinese will remain here until we establish a defensible base camp. They have given us some portable habitats and solar-powered equipment which is being unloaded as I speak. Make sure you get all of your belonging off the ship, as I suspect they will want to depart in what is to us, a few days."

The remainder of the day and all of the next were spent erecting habitat and exploring the surrounding area. Teams of four left in all directions with instructions to go no further than one mile. They were to take note of important discoveries but not to handle, eat or drink anything.

What they discovered was a pre-Jurassic period environment. Though the planet was several billion years older than Earth it was, evolution wise, primitive. No large reptiles, mammals or birds.

The teams discovered fresh water streams with water falls and fish up to five feet long; small vertebrates scurrying about; bushes and trees with berries, fruit and odd shaped nuts and plenty of firewood. The soil was dark and rich. They returned after four hours and made their reports. Ted suggested they declare quiet time and get some sleep.

Quiet times were when they were glad they listened to Ted and acquired high performance military sleeping bags. The ground was a miniature world of everything that could crawl, slither, bite, or sting. The bags were padded with small vents covered by a fine nylon mesh, making them bug proof.

Getting their biological clocks reset was tricky. Constant sunshine and no moon or stars in the sky forced people to cover their eyes with homemade blindfolds when they slept, a trick people use when traveling long distance on commercial airliners.

The next day they organized themselves like a standing army. Instead of infantry, artillery, logistics and armor, they established farming, hunting, gathering, food service and construction units and staffed them based on people's declared skills. One woman was an RN and a man an ex-Navy corpsman. They were the medical team.

That afternoon, the gathering unit left on a mission of discovery and collection. The group was led by Don Blankenbuehler who was accompanied by Tacon, Abby and Ted's son, Henry. They headed north, collecting samples of anything that might be edible. About a half mile into the forest, they came upon an area with berry bushes and large fruit trees.

Henry and I are going to collect what we can around here. Abby, your Dad told me you know how to fish. Why don't you take this hook and line and go back to the large stream we passed a little bit ago and see if you can catch something. Tacon, you go with her," Don said.

"Understand."

Abby was not overjoyed about being on a team with Tacon, let alone being with him in the woods, but she didn't complain. Soon they were sitting on the stream bank with a baited hook in the water.

"Man, there are worms and bugs everywhere," Abby said.
"Yes, good for bait," Tacon replied.

All of a sudden, a large fish, maybe a forty pounder, jumped out of the water trying to snatch a water bug the size of a Bat out of the air. It scared Abby so bad she slipped off the bank into the water. She was not a strong swimmer so she panicked as the fast-moving current started to carry her away.

"Help, Tacon, I'm going to drown."

Tacon picked up a long piece of dead wood and tried to get Abby to catch hold, but it didn't work. Partly in exasperation and partly out of concern for her, he kicked his shoes off, shed his shirt, jumped into the water and swam as hard as he could.

When he reached her, she was flailing? He got behind her, put his arm around her, yelled at her to stop fighting and started kicking his way toward the bank. He was too caught up in his efforts to save her and didn't realize his right hand had a firm grasp of her left breast. She was keenly aware of it. They finally reached the bank and crawled out of the water.

"Are you okay, Abby," Tacon said as he caught his breath.
"Yes, did you have fun?"
"What do you mean?"
"You used my situation to molest me," she said coldly.
"Sewer snakes! That's it! I save your life and all you can say is I'm a pervert. We'll, Abby Rochester, you're not the first lady or Miss America I've seen on TV. I'm tired of your insults. We will not be friends."

Abby didn't want to be unfriendly or cold but his approaches, in her mind, was disrespectful and crude at best. He had to be punished. But he had saved her life and knew in her heart of hearts that he was not trying to molest her. Besides, he's kind of pleasing to the eye without a shirt on.

Abby was a change of life baby and somewhat spoiled. She had been social during high school and college but never had a serious boyfriend. She dated and went to proms and college functions, usually with a different guy each time. She was 27 years old, tall, with blue eyes, brown hair and a head turning figure. She had been kissed many times but was a virgin, which sometimes worried her. She consoled herself by believing that the right man would show up at some point.

They sat on the bank side by side. Abby wringing the water out of her hair and Tacon tying his shoe laces. He caught her looking at him out of the corner of his eyes. He turned to apologize to her and their faces ended up six inches apart.

"What can I do to make you like me," he said softly.

The tone of his voice melted her defenses. She closed her eyes, signaling that if he kissed her, she would not be angry. He read her signal and pressed his lips against hers. He sensed that she liked it, so he lowered her down on to the grass and gave her a passionate, lingering, full mouth kiss. She swooned.

"Come on, we had better get back," he said as he helped her up.

Abby was surprised. She expected him to put his hands on her or try to get intimate. He did neither. She was completely disarmed.

The next day, the Rendinese leader announced he was leaving. Atium and Mana boarded the ship along with Terta II and his siblings, all but Tacon. Tacon faced his brother. Abby was standing about ten feet away.

"I'd like to stay. I was raised with humans and am comfortable with them. I'm bi-racial and would probably experience prejudice from the Rendinese people. I also have a friend. He pointed to Abby."

"I see. Well, I suspect this will not be the last time Rendinese visit this planet. You can always change your mind later. Be well brother. My emotions are with you."

"And mine with you, Brother."

The Rendinese ships soon disappeared into the sky.

"Abby, I sure hope you know what you're getting into," John said.

"So do I, Dad, so do I."

CHAPTER FIVE

The Edge of the Dark Side
*Place: New America, Centauri
Star Complex*

JOHN WOKE UP TO the snap, crackle and pop of what he thought were gravity engines. Adrenalin shot through his chest. It was just the sound of burning wood. The smell of coffee, something they would soon run out of and smoke permeated the air. He didn't move or take his blindfold off. His back was hurting but daydreaming was pleasant.

In his dreams he was a boy again in Virginia. His Mom and Dad had taken him to a ski resort in the Blue Ridge Mountains. He was having so much fun. His thoughts were interrupted by the feel of an arm across his chest. It was Grace.

"Morning sweetie," he said.
"Morning," she replied softly.
"Did you sleep well," he asked.
"Like a rock. I didn't realize how tired I was."

He knew he had to get up when he heard Ted announce loudly there would be a meeting in 30 minutes. Completely awake, with an energy bar in his stomach and a half cup of black coffee down the hatch, he and Grace took a seat on the ground with the rest of the group.

"I think it's time to explore our new home. I'm guessing we're about seventy miles from the ocean we saw as we landed and three-hundred miles from the un-lite side of the planet. I think we should put together an expedition of about six people. Commander Stump should lead it.

Commander, you should have a say in who's on your team, but you should take the corpsman and mostly young people who are in good shape. We need most of the skilled adults to stay here to put in a crop, to look for ways for us to make things like shoes and cloth from indigenous materials and take care of the minor children."

"Anyone who wants to volunteer, please stand up," Ed said.

Don Blankenbuehler's son, both of Neil Janson's children, Tacon and Abby stood up. All five were in their twenties.

"Great, I need to make room for a medical person."

"I think seven people would be okay," Ted said.

"Very well, bring your sleeping bags, a blanket and a coat, the closer we get to the dark side the colder it will get; a small bag of snacks and cut a walking stick. We'll depart for the ocean in 45 minutes."

"Ed, you need to keep a diary and build a map as you go. Assign names to places and things like rivers, streams, unusual topography, etc. If the group doesn't like a name when you get back, we can take a vote and change it if necessary. Look for a site closer to the ocean to build 'Polaris', the capitol of New America."

"I see we're already naming things. Why Polaris," Ed ask.

"The north star, Polaris, has guided voyagers on Earth for centuries. I want our new Capitol to be the guiding light for New America."

"I like it, you get my vote."

"Here, take this," Ted said as he handed Ed a nine-millimeter pistol with two clips.

"You never know what you're going to run in to. You're our Lewis and Clark. Good luck my friend."

Ed Stump and his team departed in the direction of the ocean. The topography was not what they were used to. A mix of hills and flat lands were covered with forests interrupted by patches of clear land. The treeless land patches were mini prairies with an eclectic mix of grasses, bushes, hot pools with bacterial blooms, geysers and moss.

Streams fed small rivers with melt water from the mountains. To the south, at a distance of about fifty miles, a range of snowcapped mountains stretched across the visible horizon. The streams could be scary places. Fish ruled the planet and many were large and fearful in appearance. Some could crawl up on the bank and try to attack you using powerful pectoral and pelvic fins like legs. Ed shot one, its flesh was quite good.

Place: Coral Sea, Proxima b

They noted the topography on the map as they went along. With no GPS or visible celestial bodies, plotting their position was primitive. A compass and dead reckoning would have to do. Finally, the ocean appeared in the distance. On the beach they gave thanks for a safe trip so far.

Ed decided they needed some serious rest. Three or four quiet times in a row. They made camp and built a fire. There were nuts, fish and a few energy bars left. Water was the only libation available.

One of the first things they noticed was there was no tide. Proxima b didn't have a moon. The second thing was a strange line of disturbed water about a thousand yards off shore.

"There's shallow water out there," Abby said.

They Built a raft out of drift wood held together with strips torn from a blanket and paddled out to the disturbed water. Ed guessed it might be a reef, which could be a good source of food fish. Sure enough, it was a reef. Ed and Tacon got off the raft and carefully walked in waist deep water exploring the reef. Suddenly a fin the size of the sail on a one person dingy appeared. Tacon saw it first.

"Ed, I think we need to get back to shore, like right now," Tacon yelled.

"Get onto the raft!"

Before they could reach the raft, the fin turned into a twenty-foot-long, two-ton behemoth with huge, armor like scales. It lunged at the raft like a Killer Whale trying to grab a Seal from a beach and with its toothless, beak like mouth, tore it to pieces. Ed and Tacon were face to face with, what a Paleontologist would call a Dunkleosteus, Devonian period killing machine.

The creature found itself grounded on the shallow reef and began to squirm, fighting to get back to deep water. Its thrashing attracted a monstrous shark that drug it off the reef. The two Goliaths engaged in a fierce battle, turning the water into a turbulent, churning circle of froth and white caps that slowly turned red.

In the meantime, Tacon and Ed had been swimming for their life and made it back to shore, exhausted but thankful to be alive. The chaos on the reef was gone, who ate who unknown.

After the equivalent of two days, they headed for the dark side. As they proceeded, the topology didn't change significantly. By the fifteenth quiet time, they were sick of fish so Ed shot a vertebra the size of a large dog. It tasted like fish.

"Hopefully, there will be something eatable in the forest ahead." Henry said.

The flat lands along the ocean, which they had named the Coral Sea after the reef, ran for 50 miles. Seeing a forest in the distance was a morale booster. It took them two quiet times to reach the edge of the forest.

Place: The great Forest, North of the Coral Sea

"Those trees look like a combination of overgrown ferns and Madagascar Baobab trees," Abby said.

They decided to scavenge for food. The agreement was that each one of them would test an item. One bite, wait an hour, another bite, and so on. The idea is if something is poisonous, biting and waiting would keep the dose low. It might make you sick but not kill you. If you didn't get sick at all, then they had a new food source.

After three quiet times, they had certified a berry the size of a plumb, a grassy plant whose base tasted like onion, a tuber similar to a Yam that grew like fruit on a vine, two kinds of nuts and the best of all, sweet tree sap. Everyone agreed the sap could be boiled

45

into a maple syrup like substance. Henry got sick eating a yellow-red berry, but quickly recovered. Abby was a different story.

"Commander, I think Abby's sick," Tacon said.

She was sitting, bent over, holding her stomach.

"Abby, what does it feel like? Do you think you could through up? That helped me a lot," Henry said.

"It's not my stomach, my intestines hurt," she replied as she rocked back and forth.

Ed pulled her arms away and noticed the crotch of her pants looked wet.

"Tacon, Henry, grab a couple of blankets, hold them up around her and face away gentlemen."

Ed took Corpsman Elliot aside and told him he thought the dampness could be blood, I need to know what the hell is wrong with her. Everyone sat quietly, waiting for the Corpsman to finish. It didn't take long.

"Well, what's going on," Ed ask.

"She'll be fine. She just needs some down time," he replied with a smile.

"What's so funny?"

"She's having her period. The pain is cramps. Totally normal," he whispered to Ed."

"Thank God. If anything bad happened to that girl, her Dad would kill me."

Ed explained the situation to the rest of the team.

"Figures, that's why we shouldn't have taken a woman along," Henry said with a paternalistic tone in his voice.

"She's done everything asked of her." Tacon blurted out.

"I know, I figured you'd defend her. You've been trying to get into her pants since we left base camp. The only good thing is her period means she's not pregnant."

Tacon, normally serious and in control, lost it. Before Henry could take a swing, Tacon grabbed his left wrist and bent it hard, creating enough pain to drive him to his knees. Just as he was about to thrust the heel of his right hand into Henry's forehead, Ed grabbed him from behind.

"Alright, cool off big guy. You've made your point," Ed said.

"Henry, if you ever insult Abby again, I will punish you severely," Tacon warned.

"Where did you learn to fight like that," Ed ask Tacon.

"Yucca flats is a boring place. My Dad taught all of his children the Rendinese equivalent of your martial arts. It was good exercise and something the family could do together."

"Amazing."

Of course, Henry's anger had nothing to do with Abby's ability as a team member. He was infatuated with her and jealous of Tacon. After Ed logged their findings, they rested and moved on. They had learned to live off the land supplemented with as much fish as they could stand. It took them 23 quiet period cycles to reach the start of the dark zone. The temperature slowly decreased as the sun appeared lower and lower on the horizon.

"Do you smell that," Henry ask.

Everyone stopped.

"I do," Abby said.

"It smells like death."

"I think it's rotting fish," Ed said.

They proceeded toward the smell and found a large area covered with partially eaten fish.

"Wow, what kind of animal could kill that many fish, Abby asked.

"No animal could do this. I think they were butchered," Ed said.

"Butchered? Only some form of intelligent life with serious hunting weapons could do this," Henry offered.

"Yes, and look at the forest and bushes. They've been stripped of anything eatable. We're looking at the mess left by a harvesting party," Ed concluded.

"That means we are not alone," Tacon said.

"Let's keep moving."

Half way to the next quiet time, they heard noises. They were in the dusk zone between the lit and unlit sides of the planet, so they could see a few hundred yards.

"Let's get closer. No talking and be careful where you step."

They soon saw a dim glow in the distance.

"That confirms it, we are not alone," Tacon whispered.

They crept closer. About a dozen men were loading containers aboard a ship. Others were tending oven like devices that spewed steam and white smoke. Another group was butchering fish.

"They're gathering food. It looks like they're pre-cooking it."

"Those are dehydrators and that's a Rendinese ship. I'm certain we are looking at a Rendinese hunting party. They could only be from Sirius," Tacon said.

"How do you know that? I thought the Rendinese were our friends," Abby said.

"They are. Terta II talked with the Rendinese leader who brought us here. The problem is the planet they colonized, Earth astronomers call it Xylanthia, orbits Sirius near the outer edge of its habitable zone making it difficult to grow food crops. Plus, the cost of colonizing their new home has been a burden. Everyone is required to give 1/3 of what they produce or grow to the government. That's created an underground market."

"But they could be legitimate," Henry suggested.

"The Rendinese leadership knows about us. They would make their presence known. No, these are smugglers," Tacon reaffirmed.

"We'd better back off," Ed whispered.

On the dark side of the moon there is no atmosphere to scatter light, so it's inky black. Although stars can be seen, they provide little back ground light.

On Earth, star shine and moon shine interact with the atmosphere at night sufficient for people to walk around carefully and nocturnal animals to see well.

From Proxima b, the stars Centauri A and B, appear as regular stars due to their considerable distance away, so they're no help. But, like on Earth, Proxima's atmosphere interacts with star light to provide a dark but not inky black environment. They were able to find a suitable camp site and declared quiet time. Soon the smugglers departed and normal forest sounds returned.

After quiet time they surveyed the area within several miles of the camp. The land was flat, free of hot pools and geysers. It was generally forested and there were streams with countless numbers of sedimentary rocks, a great building material. They also discovered an outcrop that looked a lot like lime stone. Possibly they could pound it into dust for a crude cement.

"I think this would be a good site for our capitol. Lots of food, land for planting, building materials, close to the ocean and near the dusk zone of the dark side. We can be cool or warm as desired," Ed surmised.

With a supply of food and the makings of the first map of New America, the team headed back to the original camp site to report their discoveries. It took them almost three weeks. Miraculously, no one was seriously injured. Several cases of a Poison Ivy like rash, a close call with a two-ton ocean predator, one sprained ankle, and two incidents of scalded feet from stepping into a hot water pool crusted over by mineral deposits; but nothing that would earn somebody a Purple Heart.

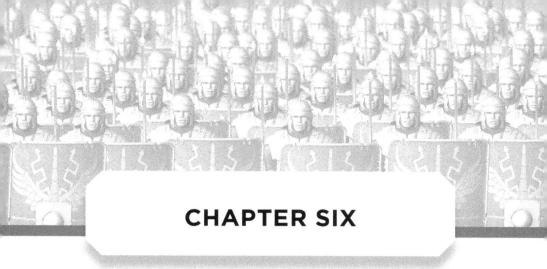

CHAPTER SIX

Trek to Polaris
Place: Base Camp, New America

ARRIVAL AT BASE CAMP was greeted with hugs and handshakes. John had been worried about Abby and was glad to see she was okay. Everyone tasted the tubers, fruit and nuts Ed brought back and they were a hit. The jerky, energy bars and similar snacks people brought from Earth had been eaten. Ed's bounty provided a break from their almost 100% fish diet.

Although Ed's team was fatigued, people couldn't wait until after quiet time to hear his report. He hung his map on the outside of one of the Rendinese portable habitats and began an oral description of the trip.

"The first thing that struck us was the beauty of this planet. Majestic mountains, beautiful fresh water streams and rivers, flora equivalent to a botanical garden and, though limited, fauna sufficient to support a human population in the millions.

The second things we learned was that traveling was necessarily slow because of the unpredictability of the terrain. There were thorn vines on the ground that can penetrate a shoe, scalding hot pools crusted over with mineral deposits hiding like land mines, waiting for a false step. Bushes and vines that can give you a serious rash. The good thing is we didn't run across any snakes or land animals large enough to hurt us.

We have identified new food items and, God knows, there is an endless supply of fish. This is the Ocean, which we named the Coral Sea because there's a big reef about a mile off the shore. There are creatures in the ocean that could eat one of us in one bite.

We then headed north toward the dark side. It's a good thing the Rendinese dropped us off at a high latitude, otherwise, walking to the dark side would become a migration rather than a safari.

On the way, we reached the edge of a forest and decided to camp and survey the area. Finding new food sources was a priority. We used the one bite at a time approach to ovoid serious poisoning. The idea is if it's poison, the first or second bite might make you sick but not kill you. If you didn't get sick at all, then we had a new food source.

After three quiet times, we had certified a berry the size of a plumb, a grassy plant whose base tasted like onion, a tuber similar to a Yam that grew like fruit on a vine, two kinds of nuts and the best of all, sweet tree sap. Everyone agreed the sap could be boiled into a maple syrup like substance. Henry got sick eating a yellowish-red berry, but quickly recovered. Abby gave us a scare when she developed stomach cramps, but it was just her time of the month."

"Was it cool on the dark side," a woman asked.

"We only entered the dusk zone and yes, it was cooler."

"About here on the map, we found an area suitable for Polaris, our new capitol. Lots of food, good farm land, a great forest and close to the Coral Sea."

"Fascinating," John said.

"There's one more thing."

"What's that," John ask.

"We are not completely alone."

"There are indigenous people on the planet," John Jr. ask.

"No, Tacon thinks they're Rendinese smugglers harvesting food."

"We think they didn't see us but we definitely saw them. So, there you have it. I recommend we begin preparation for a move to Polaris immediately," Ed recommended.

For the next two quiet cycles, other than sleeping and eating, a caravan was put together using the Rendinese solar powered farm tractors John nicknamed 'the Mules'. Each Mule had a twelve-foot long cart in which everything was loaded, including the portable habitats.

It was fortuitous that the precious seeds brought from Earth had not yet been sown. Ten acres of land had been prepared, but Ed and his team returned just in time to halt the planting.

After the third quiet time, like an eighteenth-century Conestoga wagon train, they left heading east. Tacon, Henry, and Ed acted as scouts, reporting hazards ahead and advising on the best route through the unpredictable terrain. Recharging cycles for the Mules made the trip to Polaris agonizingly slow. After the equivalent of two months they reached their destination.

Place: Polaris, New America

The first day in their new Capitol was spent erecting habitats and establishing a functioning camp site. Ed, John, Tacon and Don Blankenbuehler's son Jim, who had taken drafting courses, put together a master plan for Polaris.

They did a visual survey of the site and put a draft together using commonsense considerations. The name and location had already been agreed to. Next was the water supply, division of labor for construction of the city, common areas, crop lands and standard municipal considerations like food storage, latrines and trash disposal.

They decided to establish a commerce system where individuals would own part of the city and trade with each other using bartering. Initial ownership would be decided by the Polaris mayor and a city council who will be selected by a silent vote. John was elected Mayor because he was the most experienced survivalist in the group. The town council was Commander Stump, Tacon, because of his Rendinese connections, and Henry.

Abby and Grace were related to the new Mayor, so they were not participants.

"The town council is now in session. I've called this meeting to present the initial plans for Polaris. Comments and suggestions will be heard and considered," John announced.

Henry stood up and walked over to a large plat of the city they had hung on the side of a habitat. Henrys job was to point to things on the map as John went through the presentation.

"First, the big picture. To the east is the Coral Sea, to the North is the dusk zone of the dark side, to the south are snowcapped mountains, to the west is land future New Americans will settle and farm.

There are fresh water streams here and here. Henry will point them out. The streets will be forty feet wide and in a crisscross pattern that outlines quarter acre city blocks.

On the North end of town, we'll build a safe house for use if attacked. The walls will be ten feet thick with fireplaces and a well.

If the alarm goes off, we'll grab whatever food we have and go inside the safe house. It will also be the seat of Polaris' government.

We'll establish trash drop stations in three locations and in the center of town a ten-acre common area will be established."

"Like central park in New York."

"Yes, Abby, but not as big.

"Next was the division of labor, which was established based on ownership of barter businesses. The town council intends to deputize Tacon as Sherriff of Polaris; Commander Stump is granted ownership of Construction operations; Jim Blankenbuehler, trash disposal; Henry, Agriculture Services. Abby will own food service operations.

Each of the new enterprise owners are free to hire whoever was available. All exchanges of goods and services will be based on the barter system, wages will be paid in kind and the Government and Sherriff Tacon will insure fairness for everyone. Any questions?"

"Can people move from one business to another?"

"Yes, as long as they are not in the middle of a critical municipal project. In that case, they'll have to wait."

Stump Construction began by pounding lime stone like rocks into dust with hammers. Sedimentary rocks from stream beds and sand from the Coral Sea were carted to Polaris using the Mules.

Blankenbuehler Disposal set up trash collection stations around the compound and a compost heap at the edge of town.

Agricultural Services prepared a five-acre plot for vegetables. They had no live stock to feed, so pasture or hay production was not needed. They planted an acre of wheat for next years seed.

Rochester Food Services traded food with Stump Construction for two smoke houses and a large cold cellar dug into a hill east of Polaris. Abby also hired two hunter/gatherers.

The RN and Corpsman set up a medical clinic in one of the habitats. Everyone over ten years old, male and female, were required to find a job. When Ticon was not policing, he helped Abby for reasons obvious to everyone.

For the next six months, the New America pilgrims toiled, sweated, groaned, pulled muscles, ate, slept and made love. Three women were soon pregnant. Slowly, Polaris was being transformed from an alien wilderness into a village with form and structure. Someday it would be a city.

The ingenuity of humans is boundless. Where there is a need, there is a way. Amongst the group were ex-boy scouts, ex-military with survival training, gardeners, woman who knew how to knit and a few jacks-of-all-trades.

One man had learned to make soap from his grandmother. There was no animal fat available so he built a still, sort of a double boiler, and steamed vegetable tops and vascular plants. The resulting condensate was plant oil and water which he mixed with camp fire ashes. It wasn't the prettiest or best smelling soap, but it served its purpose.

They needed cloth for clothes, towels and blankets. Abby's hunter/gatherers, always looking for usable natural resources, found large spider webs made of strong, non-sticky filaments, almost like silk. There were also tall fibrous grasses. The spider webs were spun into yarn using a crude, handmade spinning wheel.

Salt and sponges were obtained from the Coral Sea. Wild onions and two nut varieties, when ground up, made good seasoning for food.

After six months, Ticon had not been asked to intervene in one single dispute. Everybody knew what was at stake and were on their best behavior. Then one afternoon, Abby's hunters came into town running and out of breath.

"Tacon, the smugglers are back. We're pretty sure they saw us."

"Where are they?"

"About two miles north of town."

"What did they do?"

"Nothing, they just looked in our direction."

"Alright, we have three guns. I'm deputize two men and posting them at the northern edge of town."

Tacon went to his sleep shelter and retrieved a large size container.

"What is that," Henry ask.

"It is a super Light speed distress beacon the Rendinese Ship's leader gave me. He said to use it only if we are in grave danger."

Tacon launched the beacon. Its small but powerful anti-matter thrusters came alive buzzing like a two- cycle weed trimmer and disappeared in to the atmosphere.

"Let's just hope the smugglers don't show up before the Rendinese military do."

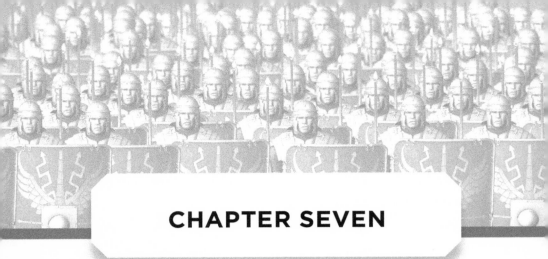

CHAPTER SEVEN

The Raid
Place: Polaris, New America

THE MIDDLE OF QUIET time is always, well, quiet. Not just because it was polite, but because everyone was so tired, it was rare for anyone to be up and about. Tacon laid still, wondering what he was going to do if the smugglers attacked. He knew that three men with mechanical pistols could not stand up to the smuggler's energy weapons.

He let his mind wonder. He had made love to Abby many times in his dreams and was about to do it again. He long ago realized he was in love with her and thought, maybe, today he might approach John about mating her. He heard the sound of footsteps and men hollering his name.

"Tacon, Tacon, they're coming!"
"Where are they?"
"About two three hundred yards from town. They're coming from the north."

"Alright, let's go," he said as others were getting up to see what the commotion was all about.

When they reached the edge of town the smugglers were waiting. Tacon fired a warning shot. Almost immediately he felt his hand burning and dropped his pistol. He'd been stunned by an energy weapon. There were about twenty smugglers. The leader approached Tacon while the rest proceeded into Polaris.

"You look like a hybrid dirt worm. We have seen mixed breeds like you before on other planets. It makes me sick to look at you."

"We are no threat to you. Why are you here," Tacon ask?

"You speak Rendinese, how did you get here?"

"We were transported here by the Rendinese military from a distant planet. We are just trying to survive."

"Then why did you release the beacon?"

"You are armed and we are defenseless."

"Are you the leader?"

"One of them?"

"This is the way it is going to be. You are our slaves. I need help gathering, preparing, drying and loading fish and food plants. Your females will cook and work like everybody else. You do as your told and no harm will come to you. If you resist, punishment will be swift and severe. Do you understand?"

"Yes," Tacon replied, knowing he had no choice.

As Tacon stood watching, the smugglers marched the pilgrims into the forest. Tacon noticed some people were missing.

"Did you leave some people behind," Tacon ask.

"Only dead ones. They were told not to resist but they chose to fight. The fauna will soon consume their bodies."

The two casualties were Commander Ed Stump and Jim Blankenbuehler. Jim died instantly, but Ed, severely burned by a high energy weapon strike, laid quietly, suffering the pain.

The smugglers put everyone to work immediately. It was like a WW II POW camp run by aliens who considered humans and half breeds like Tacon, lower than animals.

One six-hour quiet time and one meal every 24 hours. No bathing or rest breaks. The smugglers pushed and pushed. Tacon figured they were trying to finish before the Rendinese military showed up from Sirius. Their disdain for humans begat harsher and harsher treatment.

One afternoon, two smugglers decided to examine two females. In front of everybody, they held the women from behind by their arms while others opened up their tops and slide down their pants. They squeezed and probed like meat distributors examining a Colby steer.

The woman screamed for help but there was nothing that could be done. One of the women was Abby. Tacon and Henry, who both had affections for her, gritted their teeth and wrung their fists in anger and helpliness.

As one of the smugglers was about to rape Abby, Tacon could not hold back. The smuggler closest to him was so distracted by what was happening, Tacon was able to move carefully toward and behind him. He grabbed his weapon and fired at point blank range. The smuggler went down. He fired at the four smugglers holding the women. Two went down, the others grabbed their weapons.

When the rest of the captives saw what was happening, they attacked the closest smuggler to them. It turned into a full revolt. The smugglers fired as they retreated back into their ship. Tacon, Henry and two others had acquired weapons and were firing back as they retreated from the area.

"Everybody, follow me," Tacon yelled.

They ran in to the forest leaving seven people dead or wounded. The smugglers suffered four deaths. They marched for about a mile and stopped to rest.

"Abby, are you hurt," Tacon asked.
"No, just humiliated and frightened."
"They killed Ed and Jim, and we have seven dead laying back at the work site," Tacon said.
"I can't believe they would be dead if we had stayed on Earth," Henry lamented.
"This is no time to have regrets," Tacon countered.

A few moments later, they heard the unmistakable sound of a Rendinese anti-gravity system winding up.

"Help has arrived!"
"No, that's the smugglers leaving. We had better get back to Polaris. Hopefully Xylanthia picked up the distress beacon signal also," Tacon said.

Place: Rendinese Military Headquarters, Xylanthia, Sirius Solar System

It was a routine day on Xylanthia. Colonization and establishment of a functioning society was still incomplete and the economic strain severe. People were tired of the heavy tax on their good and services. The harder they worked the less they seemed to have. The Rendinese were experiencing an Earth like breakdown for many of the same reasons.

Social and economic stress was affecting the morale of the people. The black market had grown to 15% of the economy and leadership was using the military more and more to hunt down tax evaders, cartels and smugglers. It was a familiar story, too many consumers and tax evaders and not enough legal producers. People were losing faith in their leaders, financial systems and government at all levels.

The Rendinese military director, Miacon, was reviewing the latest government statistics.

"It is getting worse. Tax revenues are down again and unemployment has increased from 12% to 14%," Director Miacon said to his deputy.

"I read the report this morning. It is not good but no one seems to be going without food and shelter."

"That is because they are living partially off the illegal market. We need to do something, create a diversion, a threat to our existence, invade another developed planet."

"Or the Alpha Centauri planet we dropped the Humans off on."

"They are under our protection and using a tiny part of the planet."

"But we are pretty sure some of the dried fish showing up on the underground market is from there."

"Smugglers?"

"Yes."

"That could be our mission objective. Anti-contraband operations and protection of the human colony. Prepare a battle group for departure to Alpha Centauri as soon as possible. Troops and supplies for six moon cycles."

"It will be done, Miacon."

Before Miacon could get organized, he was arrested. He was apolitical but was a known anti nationalist. Xentorcon, the Rendinese leader, had to eliminate him in order to effectively control the military. Miacon, informed Terta II who opted to join up with Miacon. With the help of supporters, Miacon escaped and made his way to a military space port south of the Xylanthia capitol.

Using encrypted hand held communicators and the help of fellow patriots, he assembled a group of seven interceptors. To help avoid notice by air operations, they deployed using each ship's scheduled patrol time. Once they were all on station at the designated polar geostationary rendezvous point, Miacon said 'Light Off', which was the code word for transitioning to light speed and departing for Centauri.

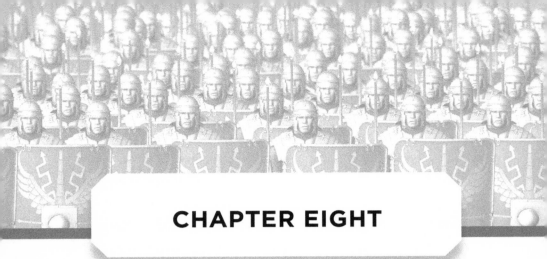

CHAPTER EIGHT

A Visit to Remember
Place: Polaris, New America

TACON AND HIS BEDRAGGLED and demoralized companions walked through the mess the smugglers had left. Polaris looked like the aftermath of a major hurricane. The smugglers had torn everything apart but seemed to have taken nothing. Grace and Abby stood arm-in-arm looking at the depressing scene.

"Mom, do you think we made a mistake coming here?"

"Honey, I worry about that all the time. What if, God forbid, we had lost you, or your Dad?

"Do you think the Rendinese government would establish a permanent garrison her to protect us?"

"It's possible, not for us maybe, but to prevent smuggling or to protect Proxima b from colonization by other aliens. Let's just hope they come. Otherwise, I fear we are doomed."

"Ticon, what do you think the smugglers were after," John asked.

"Not sure, maybe weapons or more distress beacons. When they didn't find anything, they just destroyed the place out of anger."

"Or just evil meanness."

"I don't think so. They didn't harm the children."

"We need to put together a burial detail," Henry said.

"These smugglers are a strange lot. They left the Mules undamaged; we can use one to pick up the bodies."

Commander Stump, Jim Blankenbuehler, and the other bodies were loaded into a cart and taken to a spot south east of Polaris. They had the unfortunate honor of being the first permeant residents of Polaris' municipal cemetery. The burial was not to soon as worms and bugs had already started to feast. Another couple of quiet times and the smell would have attracted the vertebras. When the last cross was in place, John said a few words.

"Heavenly father, fate is returning eight of your children. They were cherished and loved and we'll miss them. Receive them with loving arms as they return to the kingdom of God."

They all said the lord's prayer as each person dropped a green leaf on the graves. On the way back they heard a familiar sound.

"Do you hear that," Henry said.

"Yes, I do. It is a Rendinese ship coming in for a landing," Tacon replied.

"I sure hope it's not the smugglers."

"We'll soon find out," John said.

No one hide this time. What would be the point? When all the dust settled, seven ships had landed and they were not the bad guys. Tacon was delighted to see his brother approaching them.

"I am glad to see you," Tacon said as he and Terta II touched foreheads.

"And I also am glad to see you."

"You received the beacon signal?"

"Yes, one of our patrol ships intercepted it. It had a Proxima b code. I knew my brother would not send the beacon unless there was real danger. But that's not why we came. There has been a revolution on Xylanthia. Miacon, myself and the Interceptor crews are fugitives."

"What ever the reason, we are delighted to see you."

"Our resources are very meager but sit and have tea with us. We can sweeten it with sugar sap; it's better than nothing."

With the tea steeping and a small fire started, Terta II, Tacon, Henry, John, Grace, Abby and several of Rendinese officers sat in a circle talking.

"I must ask, what is the nature of your distress. It looks like a storm has destroyed the camp."

"It was not a storm, it was Rendinese smugglers. They have been coming here to gather food. When they discovered our presence, they enslaved us and abused the women. When we fought back, they killed seven of us."

"We suspected some of the contraband was coming from here."

"How's your colonization efforts going," John ask.

"Not as well as I had hoped. I think the government is trying to create a functioning society too fast. The costs have been devastating to the people resulting in the illegal purchase and sale of goods and services and poor morale."

"Sounds like a repeat of Earth's experience." John said.

"Yes, very similar and just as scary. In closed quarters, people are talking rebellion." Terta II replied.

The Rendinese unloaded their ships and set up a garrison. They'd brought a significant amount of preserved food which they shared with the humans on the first day. After quiet time, the cleanup began. The enterprises restarted their activities. The Stump Construction name was kept in honor of Commander Stump, but was now run by Tacon. With the Rendinese military present, the Sherriff's position was not a priority. After the equivalent of a month, John had a surprise encounter with Tacon.

"John, do you have a minute," Tacon ask.

"Sure, what's up?"

"I'll just come right out with it. Abby and I are in love and want your permission to mate."

"Well, I can't say I'm surprised. Your intensions have been obvious for some time. I have two stipulations."

"Anything,"

"No Rendinese free love shit. It may not matter to your people, but it does to humans. Second, it will be a christen ceremony. Abby and I will write the words."

"You forget, I'm half human. Your stipulations will be honored."

"Well then, I guess I have no objections. I know my daughter loves you."

"Thank you."

As the ranking military present, Terta II was asked to perform the mating ceremony. It would be conducted as a Christen ceremony. John and Abby wrote the words and Terta II said them. The ceremony was conducted in a small clump of trees on the east side of Polaris. Everyone, including many curious Rendinese attended. Grace was Maid of Honor and Henry the best Man. With script in hand, Terta II began.

"Welcome, we are gathered here at this time to witness and celebrate the mating of Tacon and Abby Rochester. We come together not to mark the start of their relationship, but to acknowledge and strengthen a bond that already exists. Who gives this woman away in marriage?"

"Her Mother and I," John said.

"That being said and acknowledged, we will proceed. Tacon, do you take Abby to be your wife; to live together in the covenant of marriage? Do you promise to love her, comfort her, honor her and keep her, in sickness and health; and, forsaking all others, be faithful to her as long as you both shall live?"

"I do," Tacon said.

"Abby, do you take Tacon to be your husband; to live together in the covenant of marriage? Do you promise to love her, comfort her, honor her and keep her, in sickness and health; and, forsaking all others, be faithful to her as long as you both shall live?"

"I do," Abby said.

"You have chosen to seal your vows by the exchanging of rings. Tacon, place Abby's ring on the ring finger of her left hand and repeat after me."

Tacon slipped the borrowed ring on to Abby's finger.

"With his ring I thee wed," Terta II said.

Tacon repeated the words. Abby did the same, then Terta II spoke the so important words.

"Having acknowledged their vows and celebrating them with the exchanging of rings, it is my honor, based on the power vested in me by Rendinese military protocol regulations, to pronounce you husband and wife. Tacon, you may kiss your bride."

They ate and drank Rendinese spirits for about an hour. The owners of the rings agreed to let Tacon and Abby keep them for a week. Terta II let them use his clean, environmentally controlled stateroom for a brief honeymoon.

"You have no idea how much I've anticipated this moment," Tacon said.

"I have too, but I'm glad we waited. I'm not sure exactly want you want to happen. I'm a virgin," Abby whispered as they embraced.

"Well, I have a surprise for you, I'm a virgin too, but I've made love to you many times in my dreams."

"We can make it up as we go."

"Somehow, I don't think it will be too hard."

"Hard, that's what you're supposed to be, I'm supposed to be soft," she kidded.

"You're a bad girl, Abby."

"Only for you, my love."

They took their clothes off. Both of them were nervous but excited. When they embraced, the feel of their warm naked bodies made breathing difficult. When Abby felt his manhood, he could not control himself. She wiped him off while he stood still, ashamed of himself.

"It's okay, my love. Now it's my turn. I'm not leaving this ship a virgin."

The next work period was busy. Abby had a glow that John had ever seen. Tacon attended to her like he was a personal servant. A Rendinese officer brought Terta II a message. Terta II read it. John didn't like the look on his face.

"Bad news?"

"Our frequency scanner intercepted a beacon message. There has been a coup brewing on Xylanthia. Some of the civilian leaders and a number of military ships have escaped. They are heading here. A Rendinese named Ging Xentorcon, is head of the Rendinese government and military. He is a mountain lizard but very cunning and dangerous."

"What shall we do."

"We can evacuate to Earth or stand and fight."

"We should do both," Tacon said."

CHAPTER NINE

Rebellion
Place: Xylanthia, Sirius Star System

DAILY LIFE HAD BEEN hard for the Rendinese people since they arrived on Xylanthia. They knew in their hearts that establishing a new home on an alien planet would take sacrifice, but taxes and the heavy hand of the government made them vulnerable to a charismatic nationalist named Ging Xentorcon. He promised a better way. He offered a return to dignity, wealth and the good life they once had.

Like a third world insurrection on Earth, Xentorcon's military and civilian rebel hordes systematically purged the Rendinese government and military of people disloyal to the cause. Executions were occurring every day. It was worse than Stalin's purge of capitalist or the French revolution's guillotining of aristocracy and clergy.

Xentorcon put in power a rebel government led by loyal members of the military. As a way to endear his sympathizers to the rebellion, he canceled the government's tax and tariff system that was smothering the Rendinese people. Xentorcon had a different plan. He would build a nationalistic autocracy with raw materials and food imported from other planets. They would become reapers of the cosmos. Xentorcon gathered his immediate staff together at a mountain habitat for a strategic planning session.

"Welcome leaders of the New Rendinese Empire. The planet is ours but we have much to do. The size of this planet is too small for the population. We can't grow enough food to feed everyone at a reasonable cost, nor do we have all of the natural resources to maintain our factories at high production rates.

The only solution is to acquire real estate and raw materials from suitable planets in our domain. There are a number of stars systems within a radius of 10 light years that have exploitable planets. Earth and Centauri are the obvious first choices, but there are others. We will assign these source planets a reaper number. For example, there is a star system 7.3 light years from here. We will call it Reaper #1. Any questions?"

"We will need a large fleet of transport ships to sustain such an operation."

"Yes, I have already given orders to begin building such a fleet. In the meantime, we will use military ships. We will also establish a garrison force and harvesting unit on each planet."

"We are pretty sure the people who fled with the interceptors are headed for Centauri."

"Good, then we won't have to chase them down. Prepare for departure immediately. I want two Cruiser Groups and 500 hundred ground troops. Include a harvesting unit. Families will be transported when a fully functional base has been established."

"It will be done, Ging."

"My last name only. This must be kept formal. The people will follow but they must feel that I'm above them, even fear me, while we establish the Empire."

"Understand, Xentorcon."

Place: Polaris, New America

Abby sat on a stump cutting starch bulbs and wild onions into a pot filled with a strange looking Rendinese plant stew. The prepackaged food Terta II gave them was pretty good but bland.

She was not showing yet but she was listening to her body. It felt different, her taste and smells had changed and during the last quiet time she had an upset stomach. She was sweating, so she leaned to one side trying to avoid dripping into the pot.

She looked at the sun. It was a clear day and she guessed around 90 degrees. New America was ruff and undeveloped but not a bad place to be. Sometimes she forgot about where she actually was and had to remember she couldn't walk to the deli to get a Slurpee. Memories of her brother, John Jr., rushed through her mind. She cried for him. He was one of the seven people killed by the smugglers.

Terta II was in his Interceptor attending to routine matters. Energy levels for lasers and partial beams weapons; ion engine fuel, food supplies, equipment operational status, radio signals, etc., had to be reviewed.

One set of message intercepts caused him to interrupt the routine reporting of his officers. The signals were Rendinese. He wondered if they were returning smugglers or legitimate military. They were mostly routine maneuvering and navigation signals, but several broadcasts were game changing. The messages referred to a rebellion on Xylanthia by a man named Xentorcon and that they were fleeing to Centauri.

There wasn't much talking in Polaris. People were anxious and always listening for the sound of gravity engines. They knew the arrival of an invasion force would be coming to capture the

Rendinese approaching Proxima b and Terta II's units were surly viewed as a threat.

Tacon and John contemplated the situation. There we only 25 humans left and 6 were children under age 10. If it wasn't for Tera II's ships and troops, they would be in an impossible situation. It was time for a group meeting.

"I don't think we need to discuss how and why we're in the predicament we're in. What we must do is hope for the best and plan for the worst. It has been suggested that we prepare to defend New America and at the same time be ready to abandon the planet if necessary. We have a few pistols and three boxes of ammo. The only help we can provide is labor," John said.

"Everything and everyone are important. This is the situation. We now have two problems, smugglers and Rendinese military forces. We have intercepted message traffic indicating there has been a rebellion and Xylanthia is under the control of a dictator named Xentorcon. A group of loyalists has fled Xylanthia and are heading here," Terta II explained.

"That's four entities coming together at the same time. Something will have to give."

"The Rendinese Rebels will most likely show up with at least one cruiser group. They are four hundred-thousand-ton ships that can deploy nine squadrons of exo/endo atmospheric all-weather interceptors. They are capable of wormhole travel and long-term deployment in deep space. They can comfortably carry 500 ground troops.

The interceptors are capable of endo/exo atmospheric flight; crewed by four men; powered by anti-gravity engines for takeoff and landing, chemical engines fueled with high energy liquid jell for endo-atmospheric boost and high flow cold fusion ion engines for exo-atmospheric cruising. They are armed with missiles, fusion torpedoes and neutral partial beam cannons. Each can carry six troopers. That means they can put a couple hundred troops on the ground very quickly.

I have seven ships with crews loyal to me. My three Survey ships are lightly armored and have a crew of 12. My four interceptors have six troops each. That is two dozen professional military. You have about a dozen males. Three dozen against a battle cruiser and hundreds of troops makes for impossible odds," Terta II surmised.

"What about the loyalist?"

"If they arrive on time, it would help, but I doubt they got away with a Battle Cruiser."

"Does that mean we should abandon Polaris."

"One way or another. We can't defend Polaris directly. It would be a last act of defiance that would end in our deaths or capture. We need to leave. The question is, leave to go where. Do we try to flee to another solar system, go to Earth or hide on the dark side of this planet," Terta II asked?

"You mean like, become an underground resistance group or something?"

"I think the dark side is a good option," Abby said.

"Yea, we could use the Mules to excavate a pit to bury the portable habitats. With the ship's systems shut down and us in a covered habitat, our electromagnetic and infrared signatures would be very low," Tacon offered.

"We could sabotage them and set traps."

"like the French underground in WW II," Henry said.

"Let us not get a head of ourselves. This is not a Hollywood movie. Alright, unless someone has strong objections, lets prepare to move," John said.

*Place: Rendinese Cruiser Group,
in route to New America*

Travel in deep space would be impossible with Earth's 21st century technology. Lack of a propulsion system capable of achieving super light speed is only one problem. Military and commercial vessels use Newton's simple laws of motion, the stars, gravity, and Earth's rotation as inputs to inertial navigation systems that allow travelers to follow great circle routes from point a to point b.

At Mach II, accelerations are small, so time and positional reference frames remain inertial. Stars appear fixed and the plane can be tracked with the naked eye. At super light speed a ship's navigational refence frame is non-inertial, at 10 times the speed of light, the stars move; at 50 times the speed of light near field stars become a blur to a space ship's crew.

The transition from sonic to super-sonic speed creates a sound boom; the transition to super light speed creates an optical burst after which the vessel can no longer be tracked by the naked eye.

Navigating in a relativistic time-space at super light speed makes subsonic inertial navigation on Earth look as simple as walking. At super light speed, space time is warped and, like turning an aircraft carrier at sea, course changes must be implemented long before the actual course change can be achieved.

Moreover, the course you want to travel during a high-speed run must be cleared ahead of time. Space Distort Signal Probes, capable of super light speed, must be deployed to ensure the intended track is clear.

Collision with a pea size object at super light speed would result in a super nova like explosion that would leave only an expanding cloud of plasma.

Interstellar travel necessarily becomes a series of high-speed runs and probe deployments. For the crew it's an in and out of acceleration chairs routine, including for the 500 troops on board. It's not the Queen Mary where everyone spends their time eating, dancing and romancing.

Xentorcon choose to bring one Cruiser group to Centauri. Supporting the Rebel government was critical, so he left his other Battle Cruisers parked in orbit around Xylanthia.

"Xentorcon, we will be at the deceleration point for Centauri soon," his navigator reported.

"Good, give the necessary orders when the time comes."

"Acknowledged."

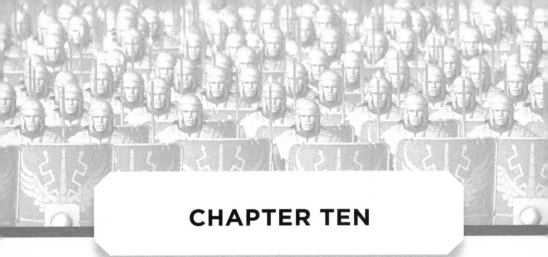

CHAPTER TEN

Pilgrims in the Middle
Place: Polaris, New America

THE COLONY WORKED IN earnest to complete preparations for moving to the dark side of the planet, all the while hoping they could finish before the smugglers or Xentorcon's ships arrived. But fate was against them as the sound of gravity engines could be heard. Fear gripped the Polaris pilgrims as they stood and waited for their fate. Preparations for moving had not been completed, so running was futile. Instead, they found hiding places in bushes and behind trees.

They could hear activity from the north where the ships had landed. Soon they heard talking. It was Rendinese but where they friend or foe.

"If you're here, show yourselves," Miacon yelled.

Only Terta II and Tacon understood Rendinese. Tacon concluded that hiding was useless and revealed himself.

"Who are you? You are not Rendinese. Are you from the indigenous population of this planet?"

"No, my father was a human from the planet Earth and my mother was Rendinese. My name is Tacon."

"I am Miacon, leader of the Rendinese military, at least I used to be. Xentorcon now runs the Rendinese empire. Where are the humans that were dropped off here," Miacon ask?

"Everyone reveal yourselves," Tacon hollered.

"There are about two dozen humans left. Rendinese smugglers killed nine of them."

"Smugglers, I knew it. They have been supplying the illegal market with food. You are lucky they didn't kill all of you."

"Miacon, I never thought I would be glad to see you," Terta II said.

"Yes, I remember you. Strong opinions but competent," Miacon said as he turned to look at him.

"I have three survey ships and three interceptors parked to the east. How many ships do you have?"

"Seven interceptors."

"You know that Xentorcon will be coming after both of us. Even together, we cannot defeat a Battle Cruiser."

"No, but we can make it painful. I suggest we set up a defense immediately. We will keep fires burning around the clock at you camp site. That will attract them initially. Explosives and close-in-weapon systems will surprise them."

"What is a close-in-weapon system," John ask.

"It is part of an interceptors defense system. They are unmanned, fully automatic rapid-fire energy weapons. You program in a sector, put them in automatic and the weapon does the rest."

"Okay, then we could set up a second defensive line half way between here and the ships."

"While you're keeping Xentorcon's troops busy, I will take three of my interceptors and attack the Battle Cruiser."

"That's a suicide mission," John said.

"As head of the Rendinese military, I was privy to certain facts, certain technical specifications. The battle cruiser is vulnerable in three places. Its ion engine exhaust nozzles, the control bridge viewing ports and the launch bay doors while they are open."

"So, if you could get hull burner torpedoes into one of those places, you could do serious damage," Tacon said.

"Yes, but there is one more possibility. The cruiser uses fire control radars for close in self-defense. In fact, they use the same frequency as the interceptor weapons we will be using."

"The jamming will affect your weapons too," Henry concluded.

"There is a possibility better than jamming. The radar's waveguides are connected to an electronic receiver which in turn is connected to the ships master computer."

"I think I understand. You're going to give the cruiser, what we call on Earth, a virus," John said.

"If we can do it, the master computer will lock up. Everything on the ship is wireless so environmental and weapon systems will cease to function. The crew has portable breathing masks that last long enough for them to reboot and clear the virus. In the meantime, it will distract them and take some pressure off of us."

"If Xentorcon lands troops, my interceptors will engage. I'll remove the incubator stations from the survey ships to make room for people when we abandon the planet," Terta II said.

"Good, if things go bad on the ground and I am destroyed by the cruiser, whoever is left should get aboard your ships and leave for Earth," Miacon said.

With a plan agreed to, hundreds of remotely detonatable explosives were buried around Polaris. Four close-in-weapons were positioned, each one programmed for a 45-degree sector. Halfway to Terta II's ships, a second defensive position was established with two close-in-weapons facing west. In the field in front of the guns, more explosives were buried.

With everything in place, quiet time was declared.

Miacon surprised everyone by retrieving a large container of intoxicant, that he called Pulp Root relaxant. Fires were kept burning continually. Soon all were asleep except Tacon and Abby.

"This Miacon, do you trust him," Abby whispered.

"I think so. We don't have much choice. How do you feel?"

"Okay, I guess. Why do you ask?"

"Well, you being pregnant, I thought I'd ask."

"That's sweet."

"Do you want to fool around a little," he asks.

"Are you trying to seduce me," she said as she put her hand on his thigh and squeezed.

"You're making it hard to breath," he said.

"I think I like this. I have complete control of you."

"You certainly have my attention. You don't have to stop that any time soon."

Abby rolled on top of him and with his face in her cleavage, finished what she had started.

"Tension gone my husband?"

"I love you, but what about you?"

"Just hold me. Why do all Rendinese names end in the letters con?"

"I attended your schools while growing up in Yucca Flats. I remember many Greek surnames end in os or no, Polish names in k or ki. Rendinese are a one race, single culture society where a majority of the names end in con. It is just the way it is."

Five hours into quiet time, Miacon was awoken by one of his officers.

"Miacon, signal traffic indicates Xentorcon is approaching."
"Acknowledged, wake everyone up."
"Put extra wood on the fires, get everyone to the second defensive lines. Select two of the humans to assist you. There are three explosive fields, each will need a detonation controller," Miacon said to Tacon.

With everyone in position, they waited. It was like quiet time but everyone was awake. Soon, they heard the sound nobody wanted to hear. Multiple Rendinese interceptors began landing and taking off dropping over 200 ground troops. The troops moved toward Polaris. The New America defenders listened to the troop leaders barking orders and the sound of their movements.

In the meantime, Miacon took off with his Interceptors. He maneuvered his units in to the line of interceptors returning to the cruiser for more troops. He squawked Rendinese military identification codes and was not challenged.

On the ground the first wave of troops reached the outer perimeter of explosives. Tacon and his assistants began the planned detonation sequence. Helmets, weapons, dirt and plant life mixed with body parts flew into the air and returned to the ground with sickening thuds.

The field soon looked like a slaughter house waste pit. Almost 75 troopers were killed or seriously wounded. Then the close-in-weapons opened up. The weapons were brutal. For a trooper, it was like getting hit with multiple 58 caliber mini musket balls. They took off arms, tops of heads, and legs. Any trooper surviving a hit soon bled out and died.

In the air, Miacon focused his 100-watt transceivers on the cruisers fire control radar domes. He began transmitting a code designed to lock up the master computers central processing unit. Assuming that would fail, he headed for the control bridge ports and fired a barrage of torpedoes. Xentorcon abandoned the control bridge and went to the backup control station.

The torpedoes were effective and within minutes hull integrity was breached. Several officers and a lot of equipment were blown out in to space. Just as the master computer closed all compartment airtight doors, it locked up.

Miacon was considering a run at the ship's ion nozzles but quickly realized the cruiser's interceptors were all returning. What he didn't know was that Xentorcon had ordered most of them back in case he needed their oxygen/argon gas supplies. Miacon headed for Polaris.

"More interceptors. We're about finished," John said.

"Get ready to abandon our positions and get aboard my ships," Terta II said over his communicator.

Miacon's Interceptors positioned themselves around Polaris and communicated to the remaining ground troops.

"Everyone hold their fire," Miacon whispered into his communicator to Terta II.

"Rendinese assault leader, this is Miacon, leader of the free Rendinese people. Xentorcon's cruiser has been disabled. Abandon your weapons and you will not be harmed."

Both sides sat quietly waiting for the Troop leader to respond. Finally, weapons started hitting the ground.

"Assemble your troops and have them sit on the ground near the camp fires," Miacon ordered.

Tacon sent two dozen of his troops to guard the rebels. There were only 56 troopers left. Rendinese guarding Rendinese. It was a sight to behold. Miacon landed and met with Tacon and John.

"What do we do now," John ask.

"I'm going to secure the weapons the rebels dropped and have them clean up this mess. We need to get the camp functioning again. We need to eat, there are wounded to take care of and we need rest," Miacon said.

"What about Xentorcon?"

"I think the damage I did to his ship will buy us some time. One off my interceptors is monitoring all Rendinese military frequencies. If he launches a second raid, we will see it coming and depart."

"Depart for where?"

"Another habitable planet."

"Like Earth?"

"That's our last choice. I do not want to lead Xentorcon to Earth where he could do unbelievable damage unless we have no other choice."

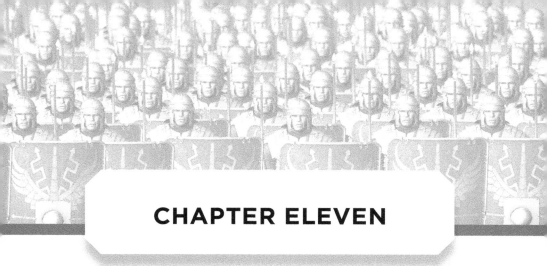

CHAPTER ELEVEN

Operation Southern Flank
Place: Washington D.C.

OVER THE MILLENNIA, EARTH has endured many emperors
and dictators who wanted to, and almost did, conquer the world.
According to Hitler's Mein Kampf, the first Reich, or realm, was
the Roman Empire, the second was the German/Prussian empire
from 1871 to 1918 and the most significant, Hitler's third Reich,
during WW II.

To a Nationalist, the white race was superior and the only one
worthy of historical mention. To the American President, Victor
Nash, Hitler's Mein Kampf was the bible. He intended to create
a Fourth Reich, which he called 'the Fourth Realm', that would
last forever. Nash seduced like-minded people at rally's, through
propaganda and by villainizing anyone opposed to him. It was a
familiar manifesto.

President Nash had been elected on a populist platform that
promised the proverbial chicken in every pot and a return to the
predepression great American society. He started slowly and subtly,

telling people everything they wanted to hear. His actions however, appealed to the worst in people.

He began to dismantle existing government agencies, ignored congress, destroyed politicians who dared to counter him and declared people of color as a threat to the country. White men were ordained by God to rule, unless you were a white liberal, then they too became an enemy of the people.

A state-run news bureau was established to counter the free press who were no longer given access to the White House. What struck fear in many hearts was his establishment of a civilian paramilitary organization, called the Red Staters, who were his boots, albeit political spies, on the ground in every county in America.

John Rochester's brother Seth found out the hard way that the consequences of saying anything negative about 'Nashism' could be harsh. Seth and his wife were having lunch with two other couples at a local restaurant. Wine loosened tongues that should have stuck to Steelers football instead of politics.

"Seth, your brother works for the federal government. What does he think about Nash." his friend Joel ask?

"I haven't asked him directly, but I think he's both scared of him and disgusted with his performance so far."

"Just between us, I think the man is crazy. He wants to be dictator of the world. I heard from my niece, who works in the Pentagon, that Nash is planning to bring home most of the troops deployed overseas."

"So much for NATO. With U.S. troops gone, rogue states will invade their neighbors for sure."

"Richard, what do you think?"

"I don't have any insider information but I don't like what I'm hearing on the news. I have a son at the university of Texas in El Paso. He told me that people are talking about the increase in military units at Fort Bliss. No one seems to know what's going on. The Army is saying it's just routine reorganization associated with base closures in other parts of the country."

"The people have to wake up or we're doomed," Seth said.

Unbeknown to them, there were Red State members sitting two tables away who heard everything. When Seth, Richard and Joel arrived at their work places Monday morning, they walked into empty offices.

"What the hell is going on," Seth asked his Boss.

"I received a call from corporate late Sunday. They said our division was being down sized immediately and I was to layoff four people. One of them was to be you. Your personal stuff is boxed up and sitting in loading dock three."

"This is illegal, you're supposed to give us some kind of notice ahead of time."

"I'm sorry Seth, I'm just trying to keep my job."

Richard and Joel told Seth later in the day that the same thing happened to them. They put two and two together. They agreed to commiserate at Helen's Coffee shop at 4:00 PM.

"Red State assholes must have done this. Did you two say anything bad about Nash to someone other than us?"

"No," Richard said.

"Me neither."

"Did either of you remember who was sitting near us on Sunday." Seth asked.

"There was a couple with kids, I think, and three young men sitting at another. I didn't pay much attention to them, but they weren't anyone I knew."

"The three men, did they have Red socks on?"

"Seth, I don't look at men's socks."

"They must have been Red Staters, Seth concluded.

"From now on, we must never talk about the government in public."

Two weeks later Nash announced he was bringing troops back from overseas. The threat to national security he said, was internal and at our borders. At the same time, people in Arizona and Texas were noticing Army trucks and armored units arriving in Yuma, El Paso and Laredo.

Leadership in the military from the 03 level up were being questioned about their political positions and loyalty to Nashism. The interviews went on around the clock. Nash wanted to create a sense of urgency. A manifesto was circulated to the troops citing the new vision for a white America. They could pledge loyalty or be discharged. They were given one day to decide. Those who pledged received a 20% pay hike and a promotion. If married, they received a 50% raise in housing allowances.

Nash News issued a warning to all undocumented people of color. They had three weeks to leave the country or be forced out by the military. The announcement caused protests and near riots along the U.S southern border. Politicians who countered NASH were destroyed by derogatory information from their pasts.

Red Staters were creating files on people and their loved ones who were viewed as disloyal. If they didn't find something, they made it up. The Red Staters set up a facility dedicated to generating fake dossiers and files. Photos were Photoshopped to show politicians in compromising positions with women and men. Eye witness accounts from people who did not exist were documented. Everyone in the country was looking over their shoulder.

Three weeks to the day, Nash shut down the border and ordered the Army to push illegals and other undocumented people into Mexico. Asian, Latino, South Americans from any country, it didn't matter. It got out of hand quickly. The Army was now dominated by racist who didn't bother to carefully check people's legal status. All people of color were swept up in the push.

At first, people resisted, but fearing for their safety, soldiers shot a few people. That caused a panic and a stampede for the border. In Mexico, the government viewed what was happening with alarm. They moved nearly 50,000 troops and armored vehicles to the U.S. border.

While the Army was clearing the border, Red Staters, now 300,000 strong, rounded up people of color from all over America and put them on confiscated AMTRAC trains. Packed like sardines, they were transported to the border where the Army took over. Nash had no special place in his heart for African Americans, but told the Red Staters to leave them alone because so many of them were serving in the military.

It took most of a month, but America's immigrant population had been reduced by sixteen million. Most border crossings were a physical mess.

"Colonel, what do we do with the bodies?"
"I'm surprised at the number. We didn't shoot that many?"
"Right sir, most were trampled or drowned."
"Have a trench dug north of town and bury them there. Use lots of lime and dig it deep. We need to clean this place up as fast as we can. Operation Southern Flank is due to begin next month."
"Yes sir."

Six weeks later, an Army Corps consisting of three infantry divisions and one armored division were positioned outside of Yuma, Arizona, same thing happened in Al Paso and Laredo, Texas. Marine expeditionary force from Camp Pendleton, California were positioned in international waters close to the Gulf de Tehuantepec, in southern Mexico. Mexico complained about the mobilization, but were assured by President Nash that they were no threat to Mexico.

Four hours after he talked to the Mexican President, Nash ordered Operation Southern Flank to commence. The Army swept down from the north and the Marines up from the south. It was maneuver warfare similar to what Hitler used in WW II. Nash thought he had perfected it by using logistics vehicles as fast as the tanks. That way his commanders would never out ran their support people. Air Force fighters providing ground support.

The Mexican government could not put up much resistance. The national Army had 250,000 troops, a small air force and no tanks. There were pockets of resistance, but for the most part, U.S. air power and advanced Abrahams tanks were too much for the Mexican Army. The biggest problem was many of the main roads were jammed with refuges heading south. Within a week, Mexico sued for peace to avoid destruction in Mexico City. Nash agreed.

The Mexican Army was disbanded and a U.S. garrison of 150,000 troops and 50 tanks put in place. The Air Force patrolled the skies 24-7 looking for trouble.

In the States, there were mixed feelings. Poles indicated that 65% OF Americans were glad the Southern border problem had been solved. 25% did not support the method but any solution was better than none.

As a way to increase the certainty that the border problem would not return, Nash built a wall across the southern Mexican border, a straight line from the Belize Gulf coast to the Pacific, cutting of a large chunk of northern Guatemala.

The United Nations called an emergency session, European leaders denounced America proclaiming it a threat to world peace.

Nash could care less. It was time for Operation Northern Flank, invasion of Canada.

Convinced the Mexican situation was under control, President Nash began staging armies near the Minnesota and North Dakota borders with Canada. Unlike Operation Southern Flank, two armies would split Canada in half, with one sweeping west to the Pacific and the other east to the Atlantic.

There was no racial component to the Canadian situation and Canada had not been a threat to the U.S. so Nash called the Prime Minister to offer a peaceful option.

"Good afternoon Mr. President. You have us worried about your intentions."

"Prime Minister, I'm not interested in war with Canada. But this is a dangerous world. I need a buffer zone around America. The Atlantic and Pacific oceans have the east and west covered. I now have a southern buffer zone. That leaves the north. The north is you."

"If you don't use force, what are you suggesting?"

"I want to put troops in Canada and missile silos in your northern territories."

"Sir, you know Canada will not accept a permanent American army presence. Canada can remain sovereign and be the de facto buffer zone we've always been."

"Not with the certainty I want and silos are critical to our defense against world-wide threats."

"Then we have an impasse,"

The Prime Minister waited for President Nash to respond but he did not. He'd hung up. Canada now had a huge problem. They had relied on their proximity to the U.S. for security which allowed them to maintained a small military. With several hundred thousand troops and seventy tanks, victory against the Americans would be impossible.

After discussions with the Canadian Parliament and the British Ministry of Defense, Canada agreed to a mutual defense pact that allowed the American military free access to Canada. It was a bitter pill for the Canadian people. They felt betrayed by a neighbor they had stood by in war and in the fight against terror.

President Nash walked into his Monday morning cabinet meeting to applause. He demanded almost God like reverence for him and absolute loyalty.

"Good morning. Now that we have secured our borders and rid the country of useless people, stabilization measures need to be implemented. This will be the beginning of the 'Fourth Realm'. A key component of stabilization will be the Red Staters. Bill, where are you on that front?"

"Mr. President, I want to first say what an honor it is to serve the greatest leader this country has ever had."

"Of course, get on with your report," the President said with impatience in his voice.

"State and county level directors are in place with over 276,000 volunteers reporting to them. Hundreds of people deemed disloyal are being arrested and moved to training camps each week. A $500 bounty is available to anyone who identifies a disloyal person. It's working very well."

"Good, how's the base relocations going, General?"

"We're pretty much on schedule sir. Navy bases will remain where they are and there is no reason to move Air Force bases. Army bases like Fort Bragg, Campbell, Hood and Benning are being relocated along our northern and southern boarders. Garrisons are being established in Mexico and Canada. US Strategic Command, with help from Navy Seabees and contractors, is preparing to put in place a line of missile sites in northern Canadian along the 65-degree latitude line."

"Excellent, these activities will provide a lot of good paying jobs for loyalists. Director, what's intel got?"

"Good morning. Nothing unexpected internationally. The rest of the world is wringing their hands, meetings everywhere, but no action. The press, of course, is running at full throttle. Nash News is countering them.

An interesting report from the Air Force about Area 51. You may recall that several decades ago, the US actually captured a real ET and one of his ships. The ship was reverse engineered and provided a lot of top- secret technology that has been shared with several fighter plane manufacturers.

The captured alien was from a planet in the Sirius solar system and identified himself as Rendinese. He had a spouse and her parents with him. He's been living in a secure facility in Yucca Flats. In 2027, ET, who called himself Terta, was killed in an accident.

About a year ago, a Rendinese war ship pickup up the remaining adults, a 24-year old son named Terta II and his siblings. We believe they headed for a planet in the Alpha Centauri Star system?"

"How in the hell does Intel know all of these details?"

"An Air force colonel, Dr. Niski, was identified by a guard at the western entrance to the DOE Secure housing complex. After serious interrogation and a few threats, the Dr. confessed. That's when it got really interesting."

"The rest of it," the President demanded.

"Apparently, about three dozen Americans left with the aliens. They were basically the senior managers at NASA headquarters. Niski chickened out at the last minute."

"Son-of-a-bitch, traitors."

"To cover up the fiasco, the Air Force logged the aliens as dying of a viral infection."

"I'm betting they'll return. When they do, I want their asses here, on their knees."

Victor Nash sat alone at his desk, sketching out a plan for phase II of his manifesto. Two years from now the Realm would include all of South America. First, he had to triple the size of his military.

He asked his administrative assistant to come in. She was a good-looking woman and knew it. The way she walked and moved could not be ignored. She took a chair in front of Nash's desk and sat down. Her shirt was too short for a business environment and she did not cross her legs. As she sat and talked with Nash, he could see the color of her panties.

"I want you to set up a meeting with military leadership and the CEOs of the top ten defense contractors. Next week would be fine."

"Yes sir," she replied.

Nash started to rotate his head as if he had sore neck muscles. She saw an opportunity and walked around the desk and dug her fingers into his shoulders. Nash was surprised but it felt good.

"You're not intimidated by me at all, are you?"

"No, I admire you."

"What's your name?"

"Sally Preston."

"You looking for favors, privileges, company or are you just ambitious?"

"They're all good, in the right proportion, at the right time."

Nash pressed the button on his desk that controlled the dead bolt on his office door.

"Am I in trouble," she asked.

"I wouldn't call it trouble. Would you object if I inspected your end of the quid pro quo?"

She just looked him in the eyes. He swiveled around in his chair and put his arm around her, mid-thigh.

"Take your top off and pull your skirt up around your waist."

He used his left hand to caress her butt and his right to massage her front. She looked up at the ceiling the whole time. He wasn't sure if she was enjoying the attention or just enduring it, a means to get what she really wanted. He stood up and ask her to sit in the chair.

"Open your mouth."
"You're too big for my mouth."
"We'll make it work."

Ten minutes later, she was dressed and left with the understanding she would become his personal assistant. Traveling with him, coordinating with schedulers, packing his bags and satisfying all of his personal needs.

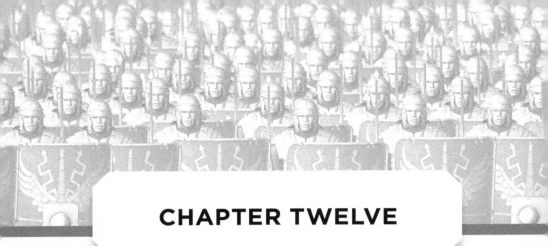

CHAPTER TWELVE

Fear and Love
Place: Thompson, Manitoba, Canada

THOMPSON WAS A TYPICAL northern Canadian town. Just over 18,000 people, a small town by American standards. It started as a mining post, but had become a provider of goods and services for an area the size of New Mexico by 2050.

Downtown had benefited from the collapse of big box stores and malls during the 2023 depression. Mainstreet was once again a Christmas card image of the perfect small town. It was lined with an eclectic mix of mom and pop businesses.

There was plenty of outdoor recreation available for fishing, hunting, snowmobiles and camping in the summer. Recreational tourism supported a healthy restaurant and motel industry. It was a town most people would love to live in.

The town would never forget the day the U.S. Army arrived. America's rude and disrespectful bullying of their longtime friend and ally made most Canadians bitter. Like scorned lovers, Canadians resisted by malicious compliance, passive aggressive behavior and silent disrespect. Most American soldiers would not eat at restaurants because the locals were spitting in the food.

Lieutenant Colonel Jeremiah Aston, Army Corps of Engineers, was in overall command. With him were two companies of combat troops, led by Major Ted Hunt, that would become part of the permanent garrison at Thompson. The new Fort Thompson would be established across the river from the town.

Colonel Aston was an army sergeant who won a scholarship to Penn State and received a commission. The military called such officers Mustangs. He was from Pennsylvania and single. One of the first things he did was establish a military social club in a leased warehouse in Thompson. The days of separate clubs for enlisted and officers had been abolished years ago.

Aston's logic was that his troops needed a safe place to socialize because the town was so unfriendly. The club provided safe food, cheap alcohol and music. With low expectations he advertised an open Friday in the Thompson Citizen newspaper.

On open Fridays, locals could get in. The catch however, was they had to get in line outside the club and wait for a soldier to sign them in. His strategy was to promote familiarity and friendship through social interaction.

Once inside the guest had no obligation to stay with the soldier who signed them in. If a soldier met a female, they could not leave with her. They could exchange phone numbers and meet at a later date. This was done to reassure parents of 18 and 19-year old girls they would be safe. Aston knew that the first 17-year old girl who was sexually abused while she was under the influence, there would be hell to pay.

To his surprise, at 7:00 PM Saturday night there were over two hundred civilians standing in line. Turns out, there were no social clubs in Thompson where young men and woman could meet. Monday morning, he received no reports of trouble, so he moved on with his duties. From time to time, he would hear of an incident. Mostly it was local men angry about U.S. soldiers stealing their girls, some unfortunately were married. He put out the word to his troops that there would be consequences for intruding on existing relationships.

Two months later, he decided to visit the club on a Saturday evening to see how things were going. He signed in the next person in line and went inside. The place was packed, smelled of beer and the music was loud. He noticed that many couples were dancing close to each other. He liked what he saw.

He bought a beer and started to sit down when a young woman approached him and ask if he would like to dance. He could tell that she was a local, not a US soldier.

"You're an officer, what's your name?"

"Jeremiah."

"That's a biblical name. I'm Mary, are you a general or something?"

"No, I'm a Lieutenant Colonel, I'm halfway up the line."

"You have broad shoulders. How old are you," she asked?

"Thirty-four, I was promoted early under President Nash's loyalty program. What about you?"

"Twenty-two."

"How come a pretty girl like you is not married or have a boyfriend."

"I'm going to be a Nun and go to Africa."

"Wow, that's a long way from Canada."

"I want to go where I'm needed most."

It had been awhile since he'd held a woman close. Her dark brown hair smelled like shampoo but there was no hint of perfume. He thought she had no makeup on, except for a little lipstick. She was about 5' 7" tall, slender in build and, he thought, had small breasts. When he held her close, he felt nothing against his chest. She was attractive but not a head turner, tomboyish, like a girl next door. Green eyes and freckles from cheek to cheek. He liked her friendliness. They exchanged phone numbers.

The next several weeks were dominated by work and Friday nights at the military club, a routine seasoned with coffee, letters from home and loneliness. Jeremiah was well known now by the citizens of Thompson but felt isolated. They were polite but quiet and careful around him. Mary was the only bright spot in his life. He liked her a lot but worried about what would happen after he moved on to the 65th Latitude missile site.

He was getting better with women but still had not developed the nerve to actually make a serious pass at one. Whether it was fear of rejection or lack of self-confidence, he wasn't sure. All of his life woman had tended to shy away from him. He suspected it was his serious as death, stoic persona. It made him seem unfriendly. He was who he was and learned to make love alone in the shower. Never-the-less, he had his Trojan in his wallet. He'd never used one, but he was ready for action.

One Friday, the club was particularly busy for some reason. He had signed in a woman only because she was next in line. He bought her a drink and they sat and talked for a while. According to the club's protocol, she was not obligated to him in any way, but she sat there anyway being nice but not really engaged. It was as if she was waiting for someone. She kept looking around.

"I don't remember seeing you here before," Jeremiah said.

"I've been here a couple of times; we just didn't cross paths." She put her hand on his.

"I'll be honest with you; I'm expecting someone else to show up. I want to thank you for being nice but I used you to get into the club early in case my date was already here."

"I get it, there's no obligation."

"It would be great if you would give up your seat when he arrives, you being alone and all." She said and looked at him with that 'I know you'll understand' look.

Just then, a cute, short girl he'd danced with once the first time he visited the club showed up at the table with a big smile on her face.

"Hi, nice to see you again, you want to dance," he asked.

"I might later, I remembered you and just wanted to say hi, talk to you in a while." She then smiled and left.

As Jeremiah watched her walk away, a man approached the table and kissed the woman sitting at his table on the cheek. Sean figured that was his queue to leave. He got up and went to the bar.

"What is it with woman anyhow, they're nice, then they move on, then they're back, never a serious flirt, is there something I say, do I smell funny," he thought.

He wished Mary would show up soon. He looked around surveying the tables.

"She's got to be here," he thought.

He continued to scan the room but didn't see her. He went to the bar to buy another beer. He turned around, out of the corner of his eye, he saw several women being escorted in. One of them was Mary. He approached her like they had never met before.

"Would you like to dance?"

"Yes, I would," she answered with a smile.

"You never told me your last name," she said.

"Aston."

"That's a nice name. My last name is Minor, Mary Ann Minor."

They danced, talked and drank a little. She was always very flattering. They danced and continued to talk and for the first time in his life, a girl he was with turned down offers to dance from other guys.

On the dance floor she kept looking into his eyes as if she was trying to crawl inside him, trying to assess him. He was seduced.

"You have strong, broad shoulders, and big muscles," she said, squeezing his left bicep with her fingers.

He just listened and said nothing. It was as if she was trying to get him to like her, something he wasn't used to and it made him nervous. What if she wants to do something afterwards, like have sex?

He held her firmly against him. She did not push away. Midnight came way too soon. When the lights flickered signaling it was closing time, they walked over to the food table and sampled several items and watched the crowd move towards the exit.

"I like you." He blurted out and as soon as he did, he felt like a school kid.

What he didn't realize was that his shyness was appealing to her. She was not looking for a cad. He was having the time of his life and didn't want the evening to end.

"You idiot, this is my club, we can stay as long as we want," he said to himself.

Then she completely surprised him.

"Jeremiah, I'm with some friends from our church, would you like to join us?"
"I would love to, thanks."

It put him at ease when she told him she had come with people from her church. Finally, he had met someone really nice.

"Come with me," she said, grabbing his hand and pulling him along.

They exited the building, walked a short distance through the parking lot and came to a black SUV. She opened the back, right door and motioned for him to get in. When he sat down, she climbed into the vehicle and sat on his lap. He put his right arm around her, she held his left hand in her lap.

He did not care where they were going. He just enjoyed the feeling of her sitting in his lap and the smell of her hair. Then he got the shock of his life. She put her lips on his and gave him the most wonderful kiss. He was caught completely off guard.

Her mouth was tasteless, not even a hint of chewing gum or a mint. He worried that he had tobacco breath. It was exhilarating and exciting. Adrenaline shot through his chest. He hoped she did not feel what was going on underneath her fanny. He tried to make it go away.

After the kiss, she rested her head on his shoulder. He was in heaven. The driver took a sharp right and pulled into a wooded area along the river. Jeremiah could see the lights from Thompson in the distance.

"Looks like we're going to the Rut," Mary whispered into his ear.

He wasn't sure exactly what that meant.

"What is the Rut?"

"It's when male Moose come down from the hills in the spring and kiss the Does."

"Are you sure you know about the birds and the bees," he said, regretting it immediately.

"Of course, where do you think we came from."

"Sorry, I wasn't trying to be a smart ass."

"When we go to the Rut, we pretend to do what the Moose do."

"I see."

He really didn't care, he was too busy hugging her, pressing his face against the side of her head and smelling her hair. He wanted to make sure there was no doubt in her mind that he liked her. The driver stopped and turned the engine off.

"We'll see you in a while," the driver announced as he and his date got out of the front seat.

Jeremiah tried to help Mary get out of the SUV. Mary resisted him.

"Is there something wrong, do you have a cramp," she whispered in his ear.

"Aren't we going to watch the Rut," he asked, a little confused.

She looked at him, her eyes inches away from his. He could feel her breath on his mouth. He found himself waiting again for her to give him a signal about what his next move should be.

"That's what I like about you Jeremiah Aston; you're not aggressive like other guys. They left to watch their own Rut so we could watch ours. Get it?"

She squeezed his forearm gently and continued to breathe on his mouth. He did nothing.

"You're either a closet Gay or you don't you like me," she said.

He though, she likes that I'm not aggressive, but is upset because I'm not more aggressive. I'm too serious and stoic. It's the same old story.

"I do, I do," he said almost with a panic in his voice.
"Then kiss me dummy."

He was feeling like an idiot. He wasn't so clumsy at work. Why was he so inept with a woman who was all but ordering him to kiss her? Maybe it was because she said she was going to be a Nun?
He put his lips on hers gently; he didn't want her
to think he really was like the pushy men she was referring too. As if she was getting impatient, she took the lead with the kiss. He escalated the kiss further. He put his hand on her stomach, sliding his palm back and forth slowly, assuming he had a green light. She was starting to breathe heavily and seemed to like it - for a few seconds.
Her reaction surprised him again. She was full of surprises. Just when he thought things were going great, she removed his hand and told him hugs and kisses only. She was setting limits for him.
They started kissing again. She responded passionately just like before. He thought that maybe she was doing what nice girls are supposed to do. Maybe it was an obligatory resistance but he should keep trying.

He put his hand on her knee, slid it up a little and squeezed her thigh thinking surely that would not be a major issue. She pushed away and slid off his lap letting her head rest on the back of the seat.

"That's it, you're making me crazy. I can tell you've been to the Rut before," she said

"No, I didn't understand at first. All I knew was that I wanted to be with you. You gave me my first passionate kiss," he rambled on defensively.

"Well, sex is for when you're married. If I didn't resist you would have touched me everywhere, and that's sex."

"I wasn't expecting sex. Hugs, kisses and a little caressing is not sex."

He wanted her to like him and didn't want to offended her.

"You say that, but if I go too far with you, you'll tire of me."

"I'm not like that." he felt like he was groveling.

"I know your sincere, but you're still a man."

"Let's take a walk," she said.

They got out of the car and walked over to the river bank. He stood behind her and wrapped his arms around her waist. He was testing to see if that was against the rules too. She didn't complain.

There were two moons, one in the sky and the other a reflection in the water. The air was still, the glow of distant lights from the town and the sound of tree frogs croaking created an illusion of isolation. In some ways he felt like he was in the country, somewhere back home or in Western North Carolina where his father grew up. He always called it the back of the beyond. She was quiet.

"You mad at me? I feel like we just had our first spat."

"No, I was wondering the same thing about you. You were a gentleman."

"Well, I want you to think I am."

He wasn't experienced with romantic girl talk. He figured she wasn't interested in Civil Engineering. She put her hands on top of his. He thought she was going to remove his hands and arms from around her waist, but she didn't.

"I have to say Mary that you're full of surprises. You really shocked me by kissing me in the club parking lot. Then you took me to the Rut and made out with me passionately. Then you shut me down. Are you sure that what you fear isn't your own desire getting out of control? I'm out of breath and wondering who is pursuing who?"

She looked at him as if he had just revealed her inner most thoughts.

"You said you liked me."

"I do, but I'm not used to a woman pursuing me, taking risks like kissing me in the backseat of a car. I'm such a clutz."

She put her finger on his lips.

"You remember Beth?"

"No, I don't think I know her."

"You danced with her at the club a few weeks ago; she and I went to school together. She said hi to you tonight, remember."

"Yes, the short girl, I didn't know her name was Beth."

"Well, she didn't dance with you tonight because she knew you were my date. She told me several weeks ago that you were safe. I came to the club specifically to me you."

"That explains a lot. Consider me conquered." He gave her a squeeze.

They continued to talk about his ambitions, her thoughts about being a Nun and collecting lightening bugs in a jar. He figured she would like stories about his childhood. The conversation ranged back and forth between silly to serious.

She was so easy to be with which gave him thoughts from time to time that he didn't want to think about. At counterintelligence training he was always told that if you're not a 10 at home, you're not a 10 anywhere else. He worried that she was a spy for a Canadian loyalist group whose mission was to get close to him.

Maybe the women lined up outside the club on Friday nights were agents. Maybe he was being played and all the people in Thompson knew it. Maybe his men were laughing at him. The sound of people approaching snapped him out of his daymare.

"Hey you two, Ruts over, got to get going," the guy driving the car yelled.

"Ok, we're coming," Jeremiah answered.

They dropped him off at Fort Thompson's main gate. He kissed her good night. He had her phone number in his pocket, life was good.

"God, what if I'm falling in love with a spy."

On Monday he was pouring over message traffic when Major Hunt knocked on his door. He and Hunt had been friends for years.

"Morning lover boy," he kidded.

"What do you mean?"

"Words out that you met a cute local girl Friday night and left the club with her."

"Yea, that's right."

"We'll, are you going to keep me in suspense or do I have to beat it out of you."

"Ski, what the fuck are you talking about?"

"Did you get any?"

"She's not like that, she's a nice girl and I like her."

"I know. Well I guess you're just not going to tell your old buddy anything."

"There's nothing to tell, we kissed a little that's all."

"Are you going to see her again?"

"I hope so, she gave me her number and I'm going to call her tonight."

"We'll if you need some advice, just let me know and use that Trojan you carry around in your wallet. If you like her, you won't get her into trouble."

"Get the fuck out of here, don't you think about anything but sex." Major Hunt laughed and left.

Jeremiah spent the rest of the day pouring over construction reports and visiting work areas, but he couldn't get Mary off his mind. He decided to do something that made him feel like a jerk, but he had to know. He asked Captain Hammond, one of two Army Criminal Investigation Command (CID) representatives assigned to his command to see him.

"Colonel, you ask to see me?"

"Yes, Captain, I need a profile on a local Canadian girl. Her parents, where she works, political leanings, who she socializes with and any connection with Canadian loyalist opposed to the Realm."

"Is this official or personal?"

"I would appreciate two things. One, be discrete. I don't want her to know she's being investigated. Second, I want you to do it personally and report only to me. Innocent or guilty, I don't want the towns people knowing the US Army is spying on them. It will just cause problems for Major Hunt long term."

"Understand sir. Anything else?"

"No, let me know the second you find anything significant."

"Yes sir."

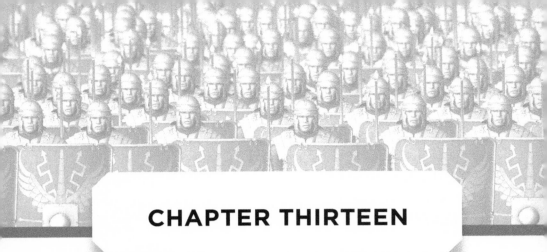

CHAPTER THIRTEEN

Operation Reaper
Place: Xylanthia, Sirius Solar System

XENTORCON STOOD QUIETLY UNDER the large pulp bush dominating the space outside his quarters. It was the only place he could be alone and safe at the same time. He was by nature high strung, suspicious of everyone's motives and used the quiet solitude of his garden to think and reenergize.

He was ambitious, intelligent and afraid of nothing. He was also an introvert who hated social engagements and diner speeches. He especially disliked and distrusted close male relationships, a very strange combination of traits for a leader planning to build an empire.

Absolute power corrupts absolutely. Xentorcon's rebellion against the government and stern leadership style appealed to the worst in some and alienated others. His ambitions exceeded his ego and he was increasingly impatient with the progress being made in building up the size of the fleet. He needed enough ships to protect and control the homeland while he was away pacifying and colonizing new planets. Loyalist felt like they were living in a near enslavement.

He walked into his staff meetings like Caesar entering Rome after defeating Carthage. He had embellished his uniform to the point where his military leaders thought he looked ridiculous. No one dared challenge him, the consequences would be swift and could be deadly.

"Reports," he ordered sternly.

"Xentorcon, Banacon reporting. We are progressing on the fleet build up. We are delivering five interceptors and three survey ships every moon cycle."

"That's not good enough," Xentorcon said, slamming his fist on his desk.

"I want that doubled and a new Battle Cruiser every six moon cycles."

"Sir, we are at max capacity. Builders are working in continuous shifts."

"Then reassign workers from domestic plants and the growing fields if you have to. The Rendinese Empire cannot wait for good enough. Assign mandatory quotas to everyone. Anyone who misses a quota will be declared a traitor and vaporized in front of the plant for all to see."

"Where are we on 'Operation Reaper'?"

"Probe data indicates there are four planets within ten lightyears of Xylanthia. Benta I, Xemain, what Earth calls Proxima b and Earth. We have designated them Reapers 1, 2, 3 and 4 respectively. We recommend that we pacified them in that order."

"Good, the Rendinese people will be kissing my feet when they benefit from the bounty brought back from our colonies."

Ship deliveries slowly increased, almost up to Xentorcon's quotas. After nine moon cycles, he felt ready to begin Operation Reaper and deploy a fleet to Benta I and Xemain.

"Welcome aboard Xentorcon."

"I'm going to the control center. Have the Fleet Leader meet me there. I want a status report."

"Acknowledged."

On board his command cruiser, the ships leader gave Xentorcon the obligatory readiness report.

"Ion engine and energy weapon fuel levels 100%, water, food supplies and spare parts inventories at 100%, no equipment casualties or sick crew members at this time. All units have reported ready for deployment."

"Excellent, deploy immediately."

The transit to Benta I was uneventful except for routine encounters with various masses traveling in all directions. The bodies raced through deep space with no predictable destination waiting for a black hole to consume them or be turned into plasma in a hyper velocity impact with a planet.

Equipment casualties, personnel problems, training and casualty drills consumed the crew's time. Xentorcon gave motivational speeches over the intercom, spoke at funerals and even performed a few marriages.

Some crewmembers were having second thoughts about their decision to join the revolution. The promotions were great but Xentorcon's increasing use of force against citizens back on Xylanthia worried them. On the other hand, if they are successful, they would surely return as heroes.

The transit to Benta I took two Earth weeks. The star was a fusion star approximately twice the size of Earth's Sun. Five planets, ranging in diameter from one-half to three times Earth's, raced around the sun in concentric orbits. Probe data indicated the two closest and the one furthest planet from the sun were sterile.

The third planet from the sun contained single-celled sea life and primitive land vegetation. It was logged into the database as an early evolutionary class planet. The Fourth planet, Berta I, showed real promise. A full survey was ordered.

The survey party departed from landing bay number two. On the way down, they noticed small masses floating at low elevations around the planet. They landed on the planets largest land mass at precisely 30 degrees latitude.

The surface environment was seductive in its beauty. Enormous trees with base diameters exceeding twenty feet dominated vast forests. Snow-capped mountain ranges 40,000 feet in height provided the background to a visual feast superior to anything on Earth or Xylanthia. Two mountain peaks exceeded the sensible atmosphere. The sky was blue with wispy orange and pink clouds presenting ever changing images

The biological makeup of Benta I was eclectic. The land-based food chain was typical of any complex, large-scale ecosystem. The large eating the small and the strongest of each species doing most of the breeding.

Reptilian creatures of all sizes and anatomical shapes dominated the terrestrial environment. It was a replica of the Jurassic period on Earth. The larger species made Tyrannosaurus Rex look like a horse. It was big reptiles eating little reptiles and sometimes each other.

The planet was rich in mineral deposits, including heavy metals and rare elements used in the manufacture of electronics. The rain forests were also a potential source of new medicines. This planet would be listed, if nothing else, as a potential new Rendinese mining and scientific station.

"Command, this is survey Team One."

"This is Command."

"As you can see from the initial data package, this planet appears to be mid-evolutionary with no intelligent life. Its flora is complex but its fauna is mostly one dimensional. The animal life observed is reptilian. No sign of mammals."

"Acknowledged, I will make appropriate log entries and inform Xentorcon."

"Thanks, I will monitor channel nine in case you need to communicate, Team One out."

The survey team set up camp next to a stream in a small clearing. They liked the sound of the water rippling gently across the rocks. It provided a soothing background sound that would help them sleep. By sunset the camp was established.

The darker it got, the quieter the surrounding forests became. Two hours after sunset, white noise from the stream and the chatter of night insects were the only things that could be heard. Sensors had been deployed out to a radius of one mile so sentries were considered unnecessary.

The steady white noise provided by the forest resonated with the hum of the camp's environmental system.

"Team leader, did you hear that," the trooper sleeping next to him said.

"Yes, yes, I think I did hear something."

"It sounded like thud."

"More like a crash," he thought.

The team leader immediately ordered a security alert.

"Seismometers in sector three indicate the source of the sound was not a single event, like a tree falling."

They noticed the brain wave signatures on one of their sensors were unusual.

"Whatever it is, it's intelligent. See the low frequency pattern on the meter."

"I see it," the team leader said as he removed the excited trooper's death grip on his arm.

"I want a patrol put together and ready to go in five minutes. Three troopers, a language transformer and a medical tech."

After making a status report to the battle cruiser, the team left for sector three. Approximately 400 yards from the camp, they came upon a massive bird like creature. It appeared to be dead or dying. The team approached cautiously. The creature's breathing was labored. It was obviously suffering.

"Sensors indicate its life functions are weakening. Brain wave analysis shows considerable stress, this creature is in pain."

"Acknowledged, keep monitoring."

Cautiously, they approached the huge bird's head. Its eye slowly opened. No one moved as the creature's dilated eye rotated in their direction.

"It's making modulated sounds. It must be trying to communicate with us."

"Any results from the language translator yet?"

"A few more minutes, the computer is having difficulty breaking the phonetics the language is based on. The creature's stress level is putting noise into its brain wave pattern but I'm making progress."

They all stood still, waiting for the tech to finish.

"I've got it," the technician proudly announced.
"Put it on the speaker," Janor ordered.
"You...cannot...help...me."

Each word the creature uttered seemed to be weaker.

"What happened to you? Are you injured or ill," the team leader asked using a microphone attached to the language transformer?
"It is...my time. Aargh...don't let the...aargh, let them eat me alive. K... kill me."
"Command, this is Team Leader."
"Acknowledged."
"I need a full medical team, ten gallons of antibiotics, thirty gallons of synthetic blood plasma and pain medication. The blood type data is on the way."
"What are you doing, treating a city?"
"I have a medical emergency with a badly injured, possibly geriatric, 8,000-pound bird."
"Why such an effort for a bird," the bridge officer asked.
"Are you ready for this, the bird is intelligent! I don't want it to die until we have completed a full interrogation."
"Yes, the orders have been given; they should be at your location within 30 minutes."

Twenty minutes later, a medical assist team was working feverishly to stabilize the creature's vital signs. The team leader continued to interrogate the bird as the medical team did its magic. A massive dose of painkiller eased the creature's agony and the presence of the landing party seemed to reduce its fear but not its confusion.

"Where did you come from," the creature asked.

"We are from a planet far from here. We are on a mission of exploration," the team leader answered.

It was not the literal truth, but the creature didn't need to know. All of a sudden, the ground started to rubble. All eyes stared in the same direction. A series of tremendous crashes, similar to falling trees and screams loud enough to wake the dead on Xylanthia, swept through the air with the force of thunder.

"Alpha-beta brain waves are all over the chart but consistent with the reptiles we surveyed earlier."

"We have a problem here. The creature's heart rate is going crazy," the medical tech said.

"Help me! It is one of the lizards. Kill me now! I do not want to be eaten alive!"

"Weapons team, I want that creature turned away if possible or neutralized if you can't. Try to scare it away with a few stun shots. If that doesn't work, you have permission to use deadly force. I do not want that reptile entering this site. Do you understand?"

"Acknowledged," several of the men answered.

The weapons team quickly checked their equipment and raced off in the direction of the sounds were coming from.

"Set your weapons to stun," the trooper in charge ordered over his communicator as they moved through the under growth.

The noise from the reptile grew louder as they progressed. All of a sudden there was silence. The weapons team froze where they were.

"What the hell, the communication tech thought, twitching her nose, trying to make the offensive odor go away.

"What is that smell," one of the weapons carriers whispered into his communicator.

"Be quiet. Fire control monocles on! Gridlock your heads up displays on my geo location, all safeties off."

After a few moments the reptile came into view. It looked like an alligator but walked upright on two huge rear legs. It had one continuous eye that wrapped all the way around its head. Its enormous tail was twice its body length.

"Now we know what the smell is. It's defecating>"

"You would need a pretty big Laser defecator to handle that pile."

"Silence on the net! Fire!"

The impact of the stun shots knocked the reptile onto its side. It struggled to get up, whipping its tail around like a farmer's scythe. Finally, on its feet, it ran off.

"It's over team." The trip back to base was short and quiet.

"Team Leader, this is weapons squad leader mission accomplished. Creature has fled the area.

"Acknowledged, report to medical for a microbe scan."

After the reptile's departure, the bird calmed down enough to continue its dialog with the Team Leader.

"My name is Sametra, which means Big Wing."

He described a society where several species of large birds had evolved into intelligent competitors. The planet was overrun millions of years ago by meat eating reptiles. Only the birds, who could escape the terrestrial carnage, survived.

"My species, the Swanhillies, grew to great size and strength. We became highly intelligent but, as seed eaters, never developed the physical attributes common to hunters

The other surviving bird species, the Owlagers, were hunters. Armed with ripping beaks and powerful talons, they enslaved us. The Owlagers built huge half-acre nests and forced the Swanhillies to keep the nests aloft, safely out of reach of ground predators.

The Swanhillies were forced to work in shifts. They were allowed rest periods to tend their young, eat and sleep. When a Swanhilly was dead or dying, it simply dropped to the ground and was devoured."

"There was never a rebellion?"

"No rebellion. My ancestor, Talenane, died like me but he did not die in vain. Your species landed and found him dying, just like you have found me. They eased his pain and learned about our situation. The Swanhillies are telepathic, so everyone knew what your people had done for Talenane, one of their most respected elders.

You freed the Swanhillies from bondage by

making the carnivorous Owlager's an offer they found attractive. You provided bouncy devices for their nest cities and helped them set up reptile farms. In this way both bird species could be safe, eat and live in peace. Some of us still fall pry to the reptiles, like I almost did, but it is rare.

The Swanhillies ask your people to erect a monument."

"Control, come in."

"Control here, report. What is your status?"

"We are heading for a monument site using directions from the alien bird."

They soon came to a clearing. At the center of the clearing was a large monument?

"That is a statue of an alien. I don't recognize the uniform or insignia."

They walked closer to read the inscription.

"Scan the inscription into the translator," Team Leader ordered."
"Acknowledged, I got it."
"Read it out loud."

'Erected by our allies from Antelya in honor of the alien called Janor who kept Talenane the elder from being eaten alive by the Big Tails and whose presence ultimately lead to freedom for the Swanhillies from Owlager slavery'

"Antelya? Do we have that place logged in our data base?"
"I already checked and we do not."
"Obviously, there are more advanced societies running around this universe than we thought. We will return to the ship. Xentorcon can decide what to do next."

CHAPTER FOURTEEN

Escape to Earth
Place: Polaris, New America

IT HAD BEEN ALMOST a year since the Rendinese attackers of Proxima b fled back to Xylanthia. Tacon and John were thinking maybe they had written off New America as too risky. Especially while they were trying to consolidate and stabilize an Empire.

However, it's hard to enjoy life when you're constantly looking over your shoulder. Every unfamiliar sound produces an adrenalin rush that causes your heart to palpitate. It was like chipmunks nervously trying to eat and sleep fearing that at any moment a hawk would swoop in silently and take one of them away in its talons.

"John, have you seen Abby," Tacon ask.

"Not since the end of quiet time."

"She might be down at the holding pen," Henry volunteered.

"What would she be doing there."

"You know she has a soft spot for people or animals in distress. She takes tree sap candy and pulp wine to them periodically," Henry said.

Just then, Abby came back carrying a basket.

"Daughter, sometimes you worry me. You need to stay away from those troopers. They're dangerous," John said.

"They're not so bad Pops, in fact several of them are very nice."

"Well, I want you to be careful."

"Miacon, I know it's been a long time since Xentorcon left but you know he'll return. I feel like we're wasting time. We must find a safer place than here," Tacon said.

"You are right. This planet is a death trap. We can leave with no particular destination and search for a new planet far from here. Such an endeavor is dangerous in interceptors and survey ships. Before we found a suitable place, we could be insane or dead from starvation. You need a battle cruiser for such a trek."

"What is the alternative," John ask.

"The only place we can go is Earth," Tacon said.

"That would put Earth at great risk."

"Do you think Xentorcon is going to let Earth alone forever. She is not that far away, is rich in raw materials, good land and a source of millions of slaves."

"Sort of like the Alamo. A lost cause but a good way to die," John said.

"Do not know what that means, but I assume it is a yes," Miacon said.

Miacon's troops and the New America pilgrims began the laborious task of gathering essential items, dried fruit, sweet sap candy and seasonings to supplement the Rendinese meals. Abby approached her father.

"Dad. The prisoners want to come with us."

"That's not something I can decide. Miacon and Tacon will have to deal with that. I'll talk to them."

John ask Miacon and Tacon the critical question.

"Miacon, what are you going to do with the prisoners?"

"I thought I would leave them here to wait for Xentorcon to return."

"They want to come with us. You can't have too many troopers, right. It's worth checking out at least," Abby said.

"Well, let's go to the prisoner confinement," John said, trying to support his daughter.

At the compound, Miacon gathered the three guards together.

"I am told the prisoners want to join us?"

"They have made such a request. Abby can verify.

"What do you think?"

"I believe them, they don't like what Xentorcon is doing and believe the Rendinese people will rise up against him. Their only worry is for their families."

"How do we know they won't rebel against us," Miacon said loud enough for the prisoners to hear.

"Our future with Xentorcon is one of hate and endless deployments. We have decided that our only hope is with you," One of the prisoners responded.

"If you make a pledge of loyalty, you may join us."

"Any nefarious activity, you will be punished severely," Tacon said.

"Acknowledged," the prisoners said in unison.

"Very well, you are free. Start helping to load the ships."

Within seven quiet times, the New America Rendinese convoy was ready to leave. Everyone except Tacon and Abby were on board and accounted for.

"Dose anybody know where Tacon and Abby are?"

"He's at the grave yard."

Tacon was saying good bye to Terta II who had died from mortal wounds received during Xentorcon's attack.

"My brother, you will not be alone for long. Spirits willing, I will return and tend to your grave. Tell father and Mother I love them and we will all be together soon."

"Tacon, Abby, we're leaving, you've got to come now," John yelled.

With Tacon and Abby aboard, Miacon issued the command to depart. Today was a special day. Miacon, normally too senior to be standing routine watches, assumed the take-off maneuvering watch because of the complexity associated with getting his rag tag fleet off the ground and into orbit.

After briefly looking at the tactical sensor display, he gave the order for his Armada to complete preparations for light speed and report when ready. Space Distort probe data indicated his first light speed path was clear. It was time.

"All units proceed to their assigned station in the sequence specified in the orbit departure plan. Guide unit is my ship."

The armada methodically formed into a single file. Each vessel departed its orbit position at precisely the moment required to ensure it arrived at its assigned formation station on time.

"All units, prepare for light speed."

Like a wagon train leaving St Louis for Donner Pass, the fleet waited for Miacon's order.

"Execute," Miacon said, which was the tactical command to go to light speed.

Place: Polaris, New America

With a Garrison on Benta I and a Scientific station on Xemain, Xentorcon sent a deep space communication probe to his second in command on Xylanthia. He did not like the response. Resistance was increasing and people were calling in sick, writing anonymous protest letters to civilian leaders. Quotas and recruitments were down. A mandatory military draft and martial law had been declared.

Xentorcon informed his second in command he approved of her actions and was proceeding with Operation Reaper and in route to Proxima b. He would deal with the insurgency back home later. The equivalent of two Earth days later he approached Proxima b with caution. His last visit didn't go well and he assumed anti empire forces were still on the planet.

He decided to send in an advance wave of interceptors. They were shocked when they encountered no resistance and saw that Polaris was abandoned. Belongings, equipment, small buildings, grave markers and garbage were scattered about. It looked like Woodstock the day after.

"Command, this is Unit Leader."
"Unit Leader, this is Command, report."
"No sign of life in the area, what are your orders?"
"Return to your ships, Command out."

Xentorcon had been deploying deep space probes in all azimuths out to ten light years. He knew they had not fled to Xemain or Benta I. The only other place would be Earth, Reaper target #4.

"These renegades must be punished. The other place within interceptor range is Earth. It's our next objective anyhow. What is the status of fuel and water supplies?"

"Ion and directed energy fuels are at 70%. Potable water if low."

"Have the survey ships shuttle water to the fleet. When they are finished and on board, we will proceed to Earth."

"Acknowledged."

Place: NASA's Headquarters, Washington, DC

NASA, like many non-national defense agencies, was mothballed except for safety and security related tasks, e.g., supplying the International Space Station crew, protection of government property and tracking of incoming threats from space like meteors and asteroids.

NASA Headquarters had been decapitated by the mysterious disappearance of its top leadership. Morale was low and many key positions were being handled by young, inexperienced staff.

Danny Watson, a GS-9 security guard was checking out the third floor at NASA Headquarters when a phone rang in a nearby office. Bored and curious he answered it.

"Hello."

"Jerry?"

"No, who are you?"

"Is this NASA Headquarters?"

"Yes, but it's 10:00 PM, nobody's here."

"Listen, I need to report some strange objects heading for Earth."

"I'm just a security guard, Mame."

"Can you get a message to Jerry?"

"I don't know a Jerry, but I'll find him in the morning when the staff comes to work."

"His last name is Miller. Tell him to call Arlene in Hat Creek, California. He knows my number. It's extremely important."

"Arlene from Hat Creek, got it."

"Thanks."

Danny's shift ended at 8:00 AM. Before he left, he checked on Jerry Miller. He found out he was a GS-14 program administrator who had been declared non-essential and laid off. The Headquarters security office had his cell phone number.

"Hello."

"Mr. Miller?"

"Yes, who is this?"

"Danny Watson, sir. I'm a security guard at NASA Headquarters. Last night I got a call from an Arlene at Hat Creek, California. She wants you to call her. She said it was urgent."

"Okay, thanks."

Jerry knew the woman's number because he was a long-time member of SETI. He had dated her years ago.

"Hello, Arlene, this is Jerry. Is everything alright?"

"I'm fine, but we've picked up modulated energy emanating from the direction of the Alpha Centauri Star Cluster. They're sophisticated signals and must be from an alien source. The only aliens we've ever encountered were the Rendinese but they're friendly. These signals are too numerous to be from one Survey ship. Can you get someone to focus the Hubel Telescope on Centauri? I'm afraid it could be a non-friendly alien force."

"I'll check on the Hubel availability. Arlene, don't get yourself too worked up until we know more. I'll get back to you."

"Thanks, Jerry. Please hurry."

Jerry knew the Hubel would take a while. He called some people he knew at the US Airforce Academy Observatory in Colorado and the Hale Telescope in California. By 2:30 PM, both of the observatories reported they were tracking two clusters of asteroid like objects.

One cluster was approaching the Ort Belt surrounding the solar system and the other one was close to the star Proxima Centauri. The closest group was maneuvering as it transited the Ort Belt. Chance are the second cluster at Centauri was not a newly acquired moon.

By 5:30 PM Hubel conformed the observatories reports. Even armature astronomers, looking for astronomical glory, began reporting the objects. It was all over the evening news.

"Hello."

"Arlene, it's Jerry. Looks like we've got aliens on the way."

"Everyone thought we were a bunch of crazies. I saw the news, what should we do?"

"There is nothing we can do. The world knows now. President Nash will be shitting his pants."

"Good, he needs a good bowel movement."

They both laughed and promised to keep in touch.

CHAPTER FIFTEEN

Words Said
Place: Thompson, Manitoba, Canada

IT HAD BEEN THREE months since Jeremiah met Mary. They stopped going to the club and went on real dates like bowling, fishing and hiking. He was pretty sure he was in love with Mary, but both of them were reluctant to fully open their hearts to each other.

"How can two stoic and private people, who are afraid to say how they really feel, build a relationship," he thought as he waited for her to pick him up.

He had a new shirt on and felt better about his appearance. She showed up in the same SUV they first kissed in. He never really got to know the couple in the front seat but Mary trusted them and she was friends with the girl, so that's all that mattered.

They arrived on time, he jumped in and off they went. She always sat close to him in the backseat of a car. It was strange; it was the one environment where she seemed to relax a little. She acted like she was his girlfriend and wanted to be held and kissed by him. Of course, he never asked her about such things. The list of words left unsaid kept growing.

He concluded that a car was the most isolated place they had available to them. Mary was a very private person, a 'for your eyes only' type of girl, so a back seat, especially after dark and with someone she trusted and cared about, made her comfortable enough to loosen up, so to speak. He cherished those times.

They went to a Cinebistro, ate Chicken Caesar salads and watched a movie. Prior to the movie, Mary endured a propaganda short about the great society President Nash was creating. It was titled the Fourth Realm. He saw she was struggling with it, so he sat quietly and said nothing.

At 10:00 PM they headed for the Ruts. He thought it was strange that the couple in the front went for a walk every time they parked. Maybe the two women had cut a deal or the other couple knew he and Mary didn't have a car and gave them priority? He thought he'd get a car from the motor pool next time.

Mary was sitting to his right. He put his right arm around her, stroked her hair a little and they began the standard 'hug and kiss session'. He was completely trained at this point; anything other than kissing and superficial caresses that lasted no more than a few seconds once or twice on any given night was the limit. Anything beyond that was like touching the third rail. Tonight though, she seemed more receptive to his affections.

After about fifteen minutes, she pushed him back and leaned against the seat. She looked at him, catching her breath, swooning with an 'oh my god' look on her face.

It didn't happen often but he knew what that amorous look meant. She had broken her own rules again and let herself get a little too passionate. He was always amazed at how much self-discipline she had. They began kissing again and at one point he tried a mini French kiss, just for a second. She terminated the kiss immediately

She was fair in her inconsistency however, if she liked it and it was within her rules, there was no problem. If it wasn't, you heard about it immediately but you earned no demerits as long as when she said no, you complied. She never got mad if you complied. He became very compliant.

All good things come to an end. The driver and his date returned and he knew that the evening was about to end. Back at Fort Thompson, they said good night.

"I'll give you a call, ok?"
"Ok," she said.

He kissed her, helped her back into the car and shut the door. The car drove off. The reason he asked the driver to stop a block away from the gate was because he knew she would not kiss him in front of the sentry. People are complicated he thought.

He didn't see Mary the following week. They talked on the phone a couple of times but with his duty cycle and her commitments it just wasn't convenient. They agreed to meet at her house on Saturday afternoon and not go out.

On Saturday, he showed up at Mary's house at 3:15. They hung around the house and actually sat in the living room watching TV for a while. That was new. Two of her sisters were visiting and the atmosphere was pleasant. They made him feel welcome and at home.

After the TV show they ate supper and sat on the porch steps talking. At 7:00 PM three of her friends walked up the sidewalk and sat down cross legged on the lawn. Mary introduced him as her friend Jeremiah. About 30 minutes later one of the women suggested they take a walk in the park. Mary said she needed to put a sweater on and headed into the house. He followed her saying he had to use the bathroom before they left.

He wasn't sure if they had a bathroom on the first floor so he followed her upstairs. No stiff arm this time. She pointed out the bathroom and went into her bedroom. He stopped at her bedroom after he finished, looked in, saw she was slipping on a sweater and decided to walk in. She didn't object.

"Nice room, I had to sleep with my two brothers when I was growing up. Two of us sleep in a double bed and my younger brother in a bunk above us. It was pretty tight."

The four of them headed for the park where they ran into a guy Jeremiah didn't know. It was one of the girl's brothers. They walked around for a while, talking and decided to sit down in a circle in a large grassy area. They talked about growing up in Thompson, mainly high school things and gossip. Jeremiah mostly listened.

"How about playing hide and seek," one of the girls suggested. Everyone agreed, the boy was appointed 'it' and faced a tree counting to twenty. Everyone scattered. Jeremiah followed Alisha.

"You're supposed to hide, "she said.

"I am, with you." He caught up with her and pulled her into a large bushy area amongst some trees. He kneeled down and pulled her onto his knee. She sat down.

"We have to be quiet," he said. Of course, he used the moment to put his arm around her and squeeze a little.

She said nothing. He knew that talking about their relationship was tricky. He was now convinced that his feelings for her scared her in some ways. He knew she wasn't ready for it. She wasn't sure what she was going to do for the rest of her life and was afraid to encourage him

He let it pass (More words left unsaid). At least they were together and he was holding her. They heard one of the girls approaching.

"Where ever you are, here I come," she said.

She must have seen them or knew that the place they were in was a common hiding place because she came right up to them and tapped him.

"You're it," she yelled and ran for her life back to the safety of the tree.

Everybody came out of hiding and they started over. Jeremiah began counting but he cheated. He watched Mary run behind some large bushes and crouch down. He intended to only look for her and instead of tagging her he was going to grab her and kiss her behind the bushes where nobody could see.

"Ready or not here I come."

As he approached the bushes, he slipped on the grass, fell but caught himself with his hands. He didn't want to mess up his new pants. He cut the palm of his right hand on a piece of broken bottle.

"Shit," he said.

She must have heard him and came out of hiding. She immediately saw that he was bleeding.

"What happened?"

"Like an idiot I slipped and cut myself."

She looked at his hand, pulled the bottom of her blouse out of her pants and tore a good size piece of off.

"Give me your hand," she ordered.

He felt no pain, just affection for this woman as he watched her wrap his hand with the torn piece of her blouse.

"You know your something else sweetie." She finished and just smiled at him.

"Sean cut his hand, were leaving everyone," she announced and they headed back to her house.

About two blocks from her home he stopped and said he wanted to light a cigarette. While he fumbled with his cigarettes and lighter using only his left hand, she knelt down on one knee in some grass beside the sidewalk and watched. He lit his smoke. She continued to stare at him.

"You know I'm crazy about you."

He couldn't believe his ears and being the man she had made him into, didn't seize the moment like Clark Gable or Cary Grant would. He should have walked over to her and told her that he was madly in love with her, took her in his arms and said all of the romantic things that would sweep a woman off her feet.

He should have told her everything she wanted to hear. He should have drug her down to St. Luke's Parish, pledged to God that he was going to resign from the Army and become a catholic, hell, if necessary, he would become a Priest. But he just looked at her like a deer staring into a spot light.

"I feel the same way about you," was all he could muster.

It was not much more than what someone would say to a good friend. His heart was pounding. The moment passed. They continued walking to her house arm in arm. After washing his hand and applying several Band-Aids, it was time to go. This time he volunteered. She walked him to the porch. They stood quietly in an embrace; two people caught up in their emotions.

Sean's hand was throbbing by the time he got back to his quarters but decided not to wake up one of the medics to take a look at it. He would go to sick call in the morning.

He climbed into bed and laid there quietly thinking about Mary. She had finally told him that she cared about him a lot. She didn't exactly say she loved him but saying she was 'crazy about him' was a major admission on her part. Why didn't I tell her how much I needed to hear her say the words? What if she took my understated response as an indication that I didn't like what she said? His mind drifted in to REM sleep.

The following Tuesday Jeremiah was brought back to reality. Major Hunt reported that his garrison stand up was complete. That meant Jeremiah and his construction and engineering units could now proceed to the missile site. For the first time in his career, he was not happy to move on. What about Mary he thought. He decided to visit Captain Hammond.

"Captain, I haven't heard anything about your investigation. Is no news good news?"

"The DIS investigator told me he's not found a smoking gun, but her brother is a member of a Canadian

Loyalist group called the Brothers and Sisters or BAS."

"Is the BAS a threat?"

"No indication at this point, but we're keeping tabs. So far they just meet and complain about President Nash."

"So, Mary is okay?"

"It seems so, but I'd still be careful. Blood is thicker than water. They know she's seeing you. If her brother or friends put pressure on her to spy, it will be hard for her to resist. She has to get along with her family, you're leaving so, the safe and easy choice for her might be to spy."

"I hope not. Thanks. If anything comes up, you know where I'll be."

He called Mary and ask her to meet him at the Rut along the river. He needed to talk with her. At 6:00 PM, she pulled alongside his motor pool car and parked.

"Is everything okay, Jeremiah?"

"Nothing life threatening, how are you?"

"I'm good, but worried you are going to tell me something bad."

"Mary, things are complicated. I have to tell you, that I love you. I didn't start out with that in mind, I just wanted someone to socialize with, date, go dancing and yes, enjoy sharing some intimacy with. I was lonely."

"Funny, those would be the words I would use to tell you about me."

He pulled her close and hugged her. No kisses, but he rubbed her back and put his right hand on her butt. With both arms, he pulled her against him tightly.

"Jeremiah, not so hard, I can't breathe."

"Did you tell me yesterday that you love me," he asked.

"Of course. Darling, for a highly educated man, you are a little slow," she said with a smile.

"You know, I will be leaving soon. I'm going to miss you terribly."

"You'll be busy and I will be sequestered in a convent somewhere. But we can visit, meet halfway from time to time."

"Is that legal?"

"My dear, I won't take my vows for many years. It takes a long time to become a Nun and we are allowed to have friends."

"I will always be your friend, but I want more."

"I know, but for now, kiss me. I must go."

CHAPTER SIXTEEN

Conflicted Emotions
Place: Missile Site, Baker Lake, Canada

TO JEREMIAH, THE 65TH latitude line was the new back of the beyond. He'd been in some out of the way places, but this would be over the top. The closest settlement to his site was Baker Lake. Baker Lake is 2 degrees latitude below the Arctic Circle and approximately 70 miles from his work site.

His construction team went to work immediately. First priority was power, lights, sanitation and living quarters. His team worked two shifts, seven days a week. He had to make the site habitable before the long Canadian winter arrived bringing sub-freezing temperatures.

The news about the astronomical sightings was met with skepticism. Most men and woman in his unit were too young to remember the UFO reports in the early 2020s and the general public was not aware of the Area 51 incident. Whether the CFL could be competitive with the NFL consumed most of the banter. The next day, a new Doctor was assigned to his unit.

"Doctor, have a seat."

"Thank you."

"Dr. Kiski, you've been in military medicine for almost twenty years, yet you're a Captain. You a Mustang?"

"No, I got into a little trouble a while ago. Cost me my rank, a lot of pay and assignment to US strategic command who sent me up here. No disrespect intended, but this is not a main stream assignment. They're letting me rot in exile until I reach the minimum retirement point."

"I must ask about the nature of this trouble?"

"I was mistakenly identified as an accomplice in the escape of some intelligence operatives held in Nevada. I told them I aided the escape because they had threatened me and my family. Authorities didn't believe me."

Not exactly the truth, but he had been sworn to lifetime secrecy about Yucca Flats.

"Well, as long as you stick to medicine, we'll be fine."

"Thank you, sir."

The next morning at breakfast, Jeremiah and several of his staff officers were eating breakfast at the Mess Hall, a large tent soon to be a Quonset Hut. Dr. Kiski approached with a full tray.

"Mind if I join you?"

"Not at all, please sit down."

"What do you gentlemen think about the President's speech last night," Major Hunt ask?

"I'm with him, but sometimes he scares me a little."

"Why's that, captain," Jeremiah ask?

"He wants too much power and acts like Hitler. I mean, what was it he talking about, the Fourth Realm, that sounds a lot like The Third Reich?"

"We'll, I'm okay with it as long as he doesn't start murdering people. I have more rank and money than I would otherwise."

"Let's talk about something more important, like the aliens."

That remark caused Dr. Kiski to stop eating.

"Aliens," Kiski ask?

"Yeah, don't you listen to the news? The aliens are coming."

"I think it's all a bunch of bullshit," Major Hunt said.

"Could be, but we know they're out there," Kiski said.

"Yeah, I heard the stories when I was at West Point. But if they're real, there would be aliens all over the place."

"Might be better than what we have now."

Everyone looked at Dr. Kiski. To disrespect the Commander and Chief was, even by inference, a no no for career Army officers. Kiski picked up on the negative reaction.

"I was kidding, gentlemen, I meant our President is so powerful, only aliens could defeat him. It was a generality, things can always be better, right."

Everyone looked at each other and began eating.

"Let's remember the rules. In an isolated environment, talking about sex, religion or politics is forbidden. It's too easy to offend someone," Jeremiah cautioned.

Jeremiah was pleased with the progress on the new base. Quarters, Chapel, and large Quonset Huts soon to be a Mess Hall and gym would soon get them out of tent city. Roads, walkways and the silo site, missile handling facility and launch control complex were being surveyed and staked. Then Jeremiah saw Mary walking from the parking lot toward his tent. He drove over to her and rolled down his window.

"Mary, stop."

"What the hell are you doing here and how did you get through the gate?"

"I told them I was a representative of the Mayor of Baker Lake and would like to make a courtesy call. Your men have been isolated a long time. Loose lips sink ships, but a smile from a woman opens doors."

"What did you really come here for?"

"I wanted to see you. Can we go inside your tent and talk?"

"Of course."

As soon as they were in the tent, she kissed him.

"Mary, why do you make me so nervous. Don't get me wrong, I liked the kiss and you know I love you, but doing what you have done is a little over the top. Does your family know?"

"Yes, they were against it but they gave me the bus money."

"Can I get you something to eat or drink?"

"Coffee with two sugars."

"Mary, I need to know why you're really here?"

Mary took a sip of her coffee.

"I told you."

"I think we are about to have our first spat. You're not telling me everything."

"What are you accusing me off," she asked as she sat her cup down and stood up.

"Mary, I'm not accusing you of anything, but I know your parents are part of a resistance group with connections all over the North America. They call themselves the BAS and are dedicated to returning Canada to an Independent and democratic state. It's a modern-day version of the Freres Chasseurs rebels."

"So, you think I'm here to spy?"

"I'm praying that you have haven't seduced me for political reasons."

"How do you know what you think you know?"

"Mary, I have people that do background checks for a living. It wasn't hard."

"So, who's the spy here? Thanks for telling me we have a traitor in the Thompson BAS group."

Mary just realized that her temper had just outed her.

"What are you going to do?"

"Listen Mary. I'm not sure if I like you right now, but I know I love you. We'll figure this out. To be honest with you, I don't like what's happening to our countries either. I was born in the wrong century. I want to return to the 20th century my grandfather told me about."

"I know, my friend, I have mixed emotions also," Mary said as they embraced again.

Jeremiah's radio was playing soft music. A special news bulletin caught his attention.

"We interrupt this show to bring you breaking news. President Nash has just announced that an alien force is approaching Earth. There position is currently near the planet Saturn. Estimated time of *arrival is 7:45 PM Eastern Standard Time. They have not responded to repeated interrogatives from NORAD. Citizens are to remain at their places of residence. The President has declared DEFCON 1. Further announcements will be made as the situation develops."*

"This is either a hoax or the beginning of the end for President Nash. At any rate, you're stuck here for the time being."

"I want to be here. I think in our heart, you are a patriot."

"If you're as devout as you say, Sister Mary to be, now would be a good time to pray."

After dinner, Jeremiah received a visitor.

"Dr. Kiski, I've got company, can it wait?"

"I don't think so. I knew it was only a matter of time before the Rendinese returned."

"Mary, would you excuse us for a moment, this could be classified." Mary left.

"You mean the aliens President Nash reported?"

"Yes, I've decided to trust you with some information that could send me to prison. That trouble I got into, it wasn't abetting Intelligence Agents, it was for helping alien prisoners held in Yucca Flats, Nevada escape along with a couple dozen Americans."

"The government, in a classified brief, said the aliens had died of a viral infection."

"Just a cover story. Remember the news story about NASA senior leadership disappearing, well they were the Americans who left with the aliens. One of them was John Rochester, who wrote the best seller 'The Cavern Club'.

"Wow, you should be a science fiction writer."

"Except this is not fiction."

"Why do you think they are returning?"

"I don't know if it's them, but they are generally friendly. Something must be wrong on Proxima b, the planet where the Americans were to be dropped off or there is trouble in the Sirius Solar system where the Rendinese settled."

"What should we do?"

"I need to communicate with a friend at the Hats Creek, California SETI site. Within the solar system, they can communicate with the aliens."

"Do they know the alien language?"

"No, but if the Proxima b settlers are on board, we can use English. If they're not, we could be in trouble."

"Trouble?"

"They could be a raiding party or worse."

"That's what you meant the other day about only aliens could defeat President Nash."

"This could be a blessing in disguise."

"Alright, I have a satellite phone and a short-wave radio."

"Perfect, we'll use both. Since I'm sure your guest has been listening from outside the tent, you might as well ask her to join us."

Dr. Kiski called Arlene at Hat Creek.

"Hello."

"Arlene, Dr, Kiski, you've heard the news?"

"Yes, they're definitely aliens. We've picked up their transmissions. There's about a dozen ships."

"I need you to use your METI system to ask them if they have humans aboard and what their intentions are."

"I've already done that. They're Rendinese and I talked to John Rochester."

"What are they going to do?"

"They want temporary sanctuary and discussions with Earth's leadership."

"Who have you told this too?"

"Jerry, a SETI member who used to work at NASA Headquarters."

"Okay, good. Send them another message. Have them monitor 25 Mega Hertz with their receivers. I'm going to call them on our short-wave radio."

"Will do."

"I should report this to my superiors," Jeremiah lamented.

"Do you want our children to grow up in a cruel dictatorship," Mary ask, as she put her face on his shoulder.

"You know how to break a guy's knee. Alright, I'll wait."

Dr. Kiski sat down in front to the short-wave radio in the communications tent. Jeremiah and Mary stood listening.

"Unidentified ships, this is Dr. Kiski, come in."

There was no response.

"Unidentified ships, this is Dr. Kiski on Earth, come in."

"Dr. Kiski, this is John Rochester. Dr., I'm surprised they don't have you locked up somewhere?"

"I paid a price but I'm still free. What happened, I didn't expect to hear from you again."

"Proxima b was not the problem. There was a revolution on the Rendinese home planet, Xylanthia, in the Sirius Solar System. A dictator called Xentorcon took control. Stupidity is not confined to the human race. High taxes, lack of adequate food and medicine, smuggling, and forced labor created the perfect opportunity for a populist nationalist to take over. Just like President Nash, he promised the proverbial chicken in every pot.

His ambition got out of control. He's turned the Rendinese Empire in to a Reaper society with the intent of pillaging other planets. He tried to take Proxima b first but was turned away by freedom fighters led by a military officer named Miacon. We decided that Proxima b was not defensible and with great reluctance, decided to come to Earth."

"You need to land somewhere remote, like a polar region or hard to get to southern Latitude. Hold for a minute," Kiski asked.

"Colonel, what is our longitude and Latitude?"

"I don't know off the top of my head. Our latitude is approximately 65 degrees."

"John, when you're near Earth, get a map from the internet. We are about 75 miles west of Baker Lake in Canada, latitude 65 degrees. Maintain maximum stealth and land there."

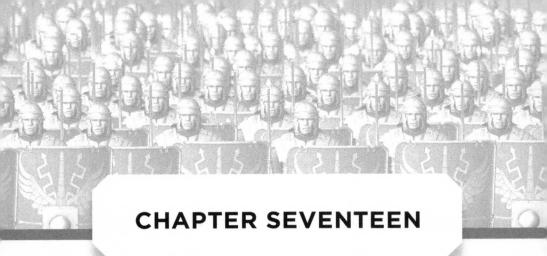

CHAPTER SEVENTEEN

Deja Vu Again
*Time: 2:30 PM, July 8, 2050, Place:
Missile Site, Manitoba, Canada*

MIACON DID NOT STAGE his landing by first entering low Earth orbit. With everything except minimum navigational sensors shut down, the basketball size radar cross section of his ships got him through the atmosphere undetected. He landed five miles north of Jeremiah's base.

The hum and whine from multiple gravity engines provided background noise for the Rendinese ships landing thrusters. Every blast blew up a cloud of dirt, small rocks, dead plants and wild life into the air. Small trees were splintered as the ships touched down.

Jeremiah sent a patrol out to greet the ships.

"Colonel, we've contacted the aliens. I'm sending the map coordinates to you now."

Jeremiah arrived twenty-five minutes later. Miacon, Tacon, John Rochester, and Abby were talking with several officers. They stopped talking when they saw Jeremiah show up.

"Greetings, I'm Colonel Jeremiah Aston, US Army and Commander of this area. You are?"

"John Rochester, leader of the Americans on board."

"You mean deserters," a Lieutenant said.

John ignored the comment.

"This is Miacon, the Rendinese leader, Tacon, and my daughter, Abby. I must say Colonel, you are amazingly calm about all of this," John said.

"We've known you were coming for a while. What are you, a survey unit, deserters, what," Jeremiah ask Miacon?

"As John told you, we are freedom fighters who want to rid the Rendinese Empire of a ruthless dictator. Unfortunately, we are not in a position to do that at the moment. Our short-term mission is to rescue your people on Proxima b and to deliver a warning to Earth," Miacon explained.

"It seems we have the same problem. Your warning is?"

"You can be certain the Rendinese leader, Xentorcon, will be coming after us and he will have no mercy on the planet Earth."

A Sargent drove up in an ATV and stopped leaving its whip antenna waving back and forth.

"Message for you, sir."

"What does it say," Jeremiah ask.

"It's from Northern Command. Be on the lookout for alien aircraft. UFOs tracked until disappearing at 100,000 feet altitude.

Be on the lookout for strange activity in your sector. Commander, NC sends."

"Orders sir," Jeremiah's adjutant asked?

"Get some camouflage netting over the ships. They are mine now, I don't want the Russians or Chinese to find them with overhead assets."

"You're protecting them?"

"The technology in those ships belongs to President Nash and the Realm. Hiding them for the time being is the loyal thing to do until I can figure the best way to connect the aliens with the President," Jeremiah said, not completely convinced he knew what he was doing.

"Let's set up enough CHUs to house everybody. Miacon, John, your welcome to have dinner with me in the Mess Hall."

"Colonel, thank you, can I bring my family?"

"Of course."

Back at his quarters, Jeremiah entered in a hurry. He was running on nervous energy pondering what to do with the situation he found himself in. He caught Mary by surprise. She was washing and naked from the waist up.

"Don't you ever knock or announce yourself?"

"Sorry, Mary. I was preoccupied and forgot you were here."

"Well, don't do it again because I'll think your doing it on purpose," she said as she put her top on.

"Let's not argue, there is too much going on."

"I like your nipples," he said trying to lighten up the situation and tease her at the same time.

She poked him in his groin, not hard, but just enough to make him bend over and huff and puff for a minute.

"Mary, you are a mean woman."

"You deserved it."

He swept her up in his arms, laid her down on his bed, spread her legs and laid down on top of her. With her legs flailing in the air and her hands pulling his hair he gave her a full mouth kiss.

"Jeremiah, please don't force yourself on me, that would ruin everything."

He got up and pulled her up with him.

"Mary, that was grab assing. If you think I would actually rape you, then you don't know me at all."
"But when you do something like that, it scares me."
"What I wish, is that you wanted me to tease you like I just did and that you trust me to not abuse your passion."
"I do, but even my father date raped my mother. She ended up forgiving him but its scary for me. Please be patient," she said as she put her face on his chest.

They stood quietly as he stroked her hair. The radio caught their attention.

"We interrupt this show to bring you breaking news. The alien ships approaching Earth have disappeared and presumed to have landed somewhere on Earth. The second cluster of objects, first observed near the Alpha Centauri Star System, are now heading for Earth. Astronomers estimate its speed, at times, exceeds the speed of light. ETA is seven days. President Nash is scheduled to speak at 8:00 PM. Stay tuned for additional updates as information becomes available."

"My God, Mary, this is becoming a nightmare. Earth can't stand up to aliens with super light speed technology. I can't even imagine the weapons they must have."

"First, it was the English in the 19th century, then Hitler, then Nash and now aliens. It's Déjà vu again and again," Mary said.

"I know, Mary. I also know that I have a bigger mission. The Missile site in of no importance now. I'm going to get a private room for dinner and invite Dr. Kiski to join us. I've already invited John Rochester, his family and Tacon. You can represent the BAS. We need to disuses how to proceed."

"So, my parents are not so bad now?"

"Mary, life is relative. Every person on this planet must now work together or we're doomed."

Jeremiah ask his adjutant to make arrangements for the private dinner. Drinks at 7:00 PM and dinner at 7:30 PM. At 7:20 PM everyone was present.

"High, it's Abby, right?"

"Yes, you are?"

"My name is Mary, I'm a friend of Colonel Aston."

"Nice to meet you. I haven't had many women my age to talk to lately."

"I have to ask, what is it like out there?"

"Travel is miserable due to the complexity of super light speed navigation. There is no night or day, no up or down, no cell towers or internet. Only when you get to an inhabited planet do things seem normal again."

"Dr. Kiski said you went to a planet in Alpha Centauri?"

"Yes, it's Proxima b. We named it New America. It's pre-Jurassic, but beautiful. Only problem is there's no night. Its rotation is synchronized with its orbit around its star resulting in permeant day time for half the planet."

"Sort of like our Moon."

"Exactly.

"You must be glad to be back on Earth. You've landed in the right spot, there are a couple of thousand young men here," she said with a smile."

"Oh, I'm married."

"Where's your husband?"

"Right over there," Abby said, pointing with her finger.

"Interesting looking man, where does he come from?"

"From Earth."

"What race is he? I don't recognize his features."

"He is the product of a Rendinese woman and a Human man. He was born in Yucca Flats, Nevada. Our child is one fourth Rendinese."

"God, you could write a book about your life and adventures."

"I might someday. My father wrote the book The Cavern Club after the 2023 economic collapse."

"Abby, you are an amazing woman. I like you."

At 7:30 PM, Jeremiah invited everyone to be seated. The dinner was Surf and Turf with a baked potato and mixed vegetables. Something for everyone, even the Rendinese. Everyone liked the ice cream served for dessert. At 8:10 PM, Jeremiah tapped his glass with a spoon. Silence was the response.

"Good evening. I want to welcome Miacon to Earth and Tacon, John, Grace and Abby back to Earth. I wish the circumstances were different, but they are what they are. Ladies and gentlemen, we must discuss the way forward. I would like to start by asking Miacon how many in his crew can speak English?"

"Myself, Tacon and four of my officers."

"That means we cannot fully integrate your people into my units. Please share what you know about the Rendinese dictator coming to Earth."

"His name is Xentorcon and he is a radical nationalist who is intent on building an empire supported by exploiting planets within ten light years of Xylanthia, the Rendinese homeland. He calls the manifesto Operation Reaper. It is a three-phase strategy. Pacify, colonize and exploit."

"That's why he's coming to Earth," Major Hunt ask?

"My assessment is he intends to neutralize your military just to make the point that resistance is futile, land troops, pacify the civilian population, punish us for treason to make another point with his troops and then begin extraction of Earth's natural resources."

"We have about a week. I know human nature; people will not just submit unless they're faced with genocide. What can we do," Jeremiah ask?

"Colonial, we have a lot of highly maneuverable platforms designed for endo-atmospheric flight. Miacon, are your weapons similar to what Xentorcon has?"

"Yes, but I have only fourteen interceptors. Xentorcon will have hundreds."

"We can't deal with energy weapons, but bombs and air-to-air missiles could be fitted to our platforms."

"Yes, that might work. Our ships will keep their lasers and particle beams. I have enough fusion bombs and air torpedoes to refit several hundred of your platforms," Miacon said.

"Okay, Mary, can you call your parents and tell them what's going on and ask them to spread the word to all BAS cells to arm themselves using anything they have. Tell them to remember the movie 'The magnificent Seven.'"

"I will,"

"The question now is, should we call the national command authorities, which means President Nash will be briefed."

"If you want instant cooperation, there is no other option. Earth must be warned that Xentorcon is on his way and we need access to your war planes immediately."

"Very well, I'll send the appropriate messages. Thank you everyone and God help us."

On the way back to Jeremiah's quarters, Mary thought she heard something.

"Did you here that, sort of a moan. Listen."

"I do hear something, maybe someone is hurt or its an animal in distress."

They moved quietly in the direction of the sound. There moon was full and the skies clear, so visibility was not a problem. Mary tugged on Jeremiah's arm to get him to stop. They were fifteen feet from two people laying naked on a blanket underneath a pine tree.

"My God, it's Tacon and Abby. Their making love," Mary whispered in Jeremiah's ear.

They remained still, not wanting their presence to be known. Tacon was on top of Abby, kissing her with his right hand on her butt pulling her tight against him. Abby grabbed the corner of the blanket and covered her mouth as she let out a muffled squeal and groaned. Mary put her hands over her ears, so she could not hear. Jeremiah was having a different reaction.

"Common, we need to get out of here," Jeremiah whispered.

Back in his quarters, Jeremiah put his arms around Mary and kissed her.

"That was especially amorous. I could feel it."

"Mary, you have no idea what you do to me. Let's get married?"

"Now, in the middle of this mess. I don't know if I want to bring children into the world we will soon be living in."

"I don't want to leave this world having never made love to the woman I love."

"Ask me again tomorrow."

"Okay, I'll wait, but in return you have to come to the Rut with me."

"Okay, how about Thursday?"

"I mean right now, in my bedroom."

"You're insufferable Jeremiah Aston."

In the morning, Mary came back into the tent with an empty coffee cup. Jeremiah had just gotten dressed.

"Morning, I thought you had returned to your quarters," Jeremiah said.

"How soon you forget. I slept with you last night. The Rut was great and I'm still a virgin."

"You're lucky I love you. It took a lot of restraint for me not ravage your body," he said as he kissed her on the cheek.

"Be patient, my love. The time will come."

CHAPTER EIGHTEEN

Duel Nemesis
*Time: 8:15 AM, July 9, 2050, Place:
White House, Washington, DC*

PRESIDENT NASH STOOD IN his oval office looking at the Washington monument. He thought George Washington was a fool because he could have been anointed King of America, but turned it down. Because of him, he rationalized, I have to deal with a government where it's impossible to get anything done without endless hearings, briefings, and quid pro quos.

He was glad to receive the news from the Chairman Joint Chiefs, that the first group of aliens had been found in Canada and that a larger force was on its way. This was the crisis he needed to take complete control of the Fourth Realm.

Jeremiah had finally reported the location of the aliens to his superiors. Nash decided not to approve the Armies recommendation to have hundreds of tactical fighters flown to air fields in Manitoba, Canada for refitting with alien weapons.

"If the Rendinese leader of the Armada is a powerful dictator, as has been reported, he and I will get along fine. Cooperating with the renegade aliens in Canada would be a provocation.

In return for helping me expand the Fourth Realm, I can vector him to the aliens he's chasing and offer a treaty that provides the resources he needs." Nash thought.

"Sally, get the Chairman, Joint Chiefs of Staff on the line."
"Yes sir."

Ten minutes later General Dixon was on the line.

"General, go to DEFCON 4."
"Mr. President, we have what could be an alien invasion force approaching Earth. We should be at DEFCON 1 and sending tac air to Manitoba for refitting. I've talked with Colonel Aston and I believe him. I have satellite phone pictures of the alien ships parked near his missile site."
"I want no provocations. I intend to work with the aliens and negotiate a deal.

Place: Missile Site, Manitoba, Canada

Jeremiah was nervously waiting for word from his superiors on when and where they were sending the fighters he'd requested. Once he knew which air bases they were going to use, he could tell Miacon where to send his ships.

"Why are they wasting time. I don't understand," he said in frustration.

"Miacon said it would take two to three days to refit our planes. We might need a plan B," Mary offered.

"I'll set up a staff meeting."

"I have an idea," Mary said.

"I'm listening."

"Many Canadian military personnel are part of the BAS and we have sympathizers around the world who hate Nash. They might be able to get us the fighters."

Jeremiah's satellite phone rang.

"Colonel Aston."

"Colonel, this is General Nanos. The President has ordered a stand down. He intends to negotiate with the aliens and wants no provocations."

"Meaning no fighters will be provided?"

"That's correct. I recommend you prepare your command for the worst."

"Very well, understood sir and thanks."

"Well, Mary, I think we're on our own."

Jeremiah sent for Miacon, Tacon and John Rochester.

"Gentlemen, President Nash is not going to help us. He intends to negotiate with Xentorcon."

"Your President is a fool. Xentorcon will not negotiate. I must consider leaving Earth. I fear you are doomed," Miacon said.

"There may still be a way."

"What is that, Colonel?"

"Mary says the resistance, the Brothers and Sisters, have cells all over North America with members in high military positions. They may be able to help us."

"I'll give you a day, then I must depart."

"Fair enough. Mary, have your father put out the word that we need several hundred fighters. Send them to major air fields in

157

Manitoba. Places like Portage La Prairie and find out if there are allies in Strategic Command."

"Why Strategic Command?"

"Long range nukes, we need some way to get the fuses in ICBMs modified. If they had proximity fuses, we could use them against Xentorcon."

"That would be an almost impossible thing to do undetected. Nash would immediately lock down silos and most of the submarine launched ballistic missiles are at sea."

"Clever people can do amazing things. At least ask them to try."

"I will," Mary said.

At 3:30 AM, Mary received a call. She recognized the number.

"Dad, are you okay?"

"Yes, love you honey."

"Love you too Dad. What's happening?"

"There will be thirty Royal Canadian Air Force jets landing in the morning at Portage La Prairie. Others will be going to Holberg and Cold Lake."

"Daddy, I know you're going to think I'm crazy, but they want the BAS to try to get ICBMs modified for near space proximity fusing."

"I don't know how that could be done in a couple of days."

"They ask me to ask you to at least put the word out."

"I will, but don't count on anything happening."

"Love you Dad and tell Mom I love her."

"Love you too."

"Well, you heard the conversation. It's Portage, Holberg and Cold lake."

"I'm getting dressed, we have work to do."

Jeremiah didn't wait until morning. He assigned three of his helicopter pilots to Miacon with a map and GPS receiver. Miacon's Interceptors would be sent to Portage, Holberg and Cold Lake respectively. Two of the bases were not the closest to Fort Thompson, but according to Mary's father, they were under control of BAS members and safe. Jeremiah called Major Hunt.

"Major, I'm going to Portage La Prairie with Miacon. One of the alien ships will be dropping off woman and children at Fort Thompson."

"Very well sir."

"I recommend you dig in and set up a defensive perimeter. You don't have any heavy weapons, but there are two truck loads of construction dynamite. In the end, Xentorcon may not care about a remote place like northern Manitoba, but I wouldn't bet on it."

"I'll do what I can. Good luck, Colonel."

"Same to you."

Place: Portage La Prairie, Manitoba, Canada

Time: 0134 hours, July 10, 2050

Jeremiah sat watching the lights from Portage Air base come into view. He could see the lights from a line of planes coming for landing. He assumed they were fighters. The BAS put out the word to all units to maintain maximum stealth, subsonic flight only, radio silence, no airborne sensors; only GPS receivers, maps and a compass were permitted.

"Portage, this is Baker Lake. Request landing instructions."

"Baker Lake, this is Portage Control, vector 087

degrees, descend to 5,000 feet. Runway L1, use the south tarmac, over."

"Roger, descending to 5,000, ETA tarmac 12 minutes."

Baker Lake was the code word agreed to with the BAS for the alien flight group. Landing was completed successfully. They were greeted by Canadian military officers.

"Welcome to Portage. I'm the Air Operations Officer."

"Thank you, I'm Colonel Astor, U.S Army, this is Miacon, Tacon and his wife Abby and my BAS interface, Mary. We need to get started immediately."

"We've reconfigured two hangers. Weapons handlers and transporters are on their way."

"Good, we have maybe three days to complete the rearming."

"What do we do when we're done?"

"Nothing, we wait. A first strike would be futile. We'll wait to see what the Aliens do, then act accordingly. The other two groups at Holberg and Cold Lake have the same orders."

"Mary, we need to check with the BAS. I need to know if anything is happening with the nukes."

Mary dialed up her father and handed the phone to Jeremiah.

"Mr. Minor, we're rearming the fighters as we speak. Any progress on the ballistic missiles?"

"The submarines are a no go. Too hard and no time. One ICBM Wing at Warren AFB agreed to turn the other cheek, so to speak. The Commander and enough of his staff were able to take control. Staff not willing to cooperate have been taken into custody.

The biggest problem, modifying the fuses, may have been solved. Fusing Engineers from Sandia National Laboratory with replacement fuses are being flown to Cheyenne Regional Airport and then transported to Warren AFB."

"Excellent news. Keep Mary informed and thanks."

Place: Fort Thompson, Manitoba, Canada

*Time: 0530 hours, July 10, 2050

In the predawn moonlight Major Hunt stood quietly pondering the future. Never in his wildest dreams did he think his army career would include combating tyranny from his own government. The thought that someday America would be under the control of a virtual dictator and at the same time, be faced with an ET invasion, was simply inconceivable.

Blended clichés were not normally part of his thought process, but his summary of the situation was grim. He and many others were about to engage in a last stand; the proverbial unstoppable force against an immoveable object. One enemy is bad enough, but duel nemeses, we'll, it was almost too much.

He was worried about and missed his wife. They had courted for six years before they were married two years ago. Duty and deployments kept them apart often. In two years of marriage, they had been with each other a total of four months. He couldn't resist calling her. It was 4:00 AM. He knew it would alarm her but time and urgency were of the essence.

"Hello," a sleepy voice answered.

"Honey, this is Ted. Sorry to wake you, but I had to talk to you."

"Are you alright?"

"I'm fine. Things are going to get crazy in a couple of days. I will call when I can. I miss you so much."

"I miss you too. What should I do?"

"Nothing, stay where you are sweetie, there is no place to go. I'll be in touch when I can. Love you."

"Love you too."

"Bye."

Major Hunt grabbed a thermos of coffee and headed for the Inner Defense perimeter.

"Morning, Major."

"Morning, Lieutenant. How's things going?"

"We've buried half a truck load of dynamite in the outer perimeter, a full load in the second and are about finished with the inner perimeter. We have control bunkers dug in behind each perimeter. When they have blown all the dynamite in the first, they'll fall back and do the same at the second and so forth."

"What about the survey drones?"

"Three are operational and fitted with five sticks of dynamite each. Major, what are our chances?"

"If everything that has been reported is true, not good. But as Colonel Aston told me, the aliens may not care about us. We're no real threat to them and we're isolated. If you're a man of faith, now would be a good time to pray."

CHAPTER NINETEEN

Prelude to Infamy
Place: White House, Washington, DC

Time: 0830 hours, July 10, 2050,

ROUND THE CLOCK COVERAGE of the approaching alien armada consumed the News media. Analysis and speculation by pundits and consultants about survival strategies and concerns about President Nash's lack of preparation dominated the reporting. The President assured citizens he had everything under control and there was nothing to fear.

"Mr. President, sources around the realm are saying people are close to panicking."

"Sally, I have a press conference scheduled for 1:00 PM. I'll address the issue again. I'm more concerned about what I'm hearing about citizens. civilians are ignoring curfews; Red State members are not showing up for meetings and parts of the military is being relocated for no apparent reason. Government vehicles are breaking down, running out of gas and pilfering has increased."

"Maybe people are thinking the aliens are going to destroy us, so what the hell, might as well look out for myself," Sally suggested.

"As citizens of the Realm, their safety is my responsibility," he said loudly as he slammed his fist on the desk.

"See this. What's that all about. A Red State leader in Winnipeg, Canada reports army units and military aircraft are being reassigned," he said angrily as he slapped the memo on his desk in front of Sally.

"I can have the chief of staff make some calls."

"Do it! It's time I sent a message. I'm going to declare martial law."

Sally Preston, a covert BAS plant, prepared a memo to the Chairman, Joint Chiefs of staff, saying the President will declare martial law at 1200 hours EST, July 10, 2050. He wants every county and province in the Realm to be locked down ASAP. With the help of staffers, a set of directives was developed:

(1) Inhabitants must be in doors by 2300 hours local time and must not leave their homes before 0600 hours.

(2) Personal weapons and ammunition must be turned in immediately.

(3) Orders given by the military are to be strictly obeyed.

(4) Persons committing acts of subversion will be arrested along with their family and immediate neighbors.

"This is good Sally, send it. I just received another message from a Red Stater in a place called Portage La Prairie. It's in Canada. She says Canadian fighter aircraft have been landing all morning. She can see them from the porch of her house. I want that investigated."

"Yes sir."

After Sally was sure the message and appropriate phone calls were made, she excused herself and left the white house. On Pennsylvania Avenue, she made a phone call to the local BAS. They would know what to do.

Place: Xentorcon's Armada

Time: 1346 hours, July 10, 2050,

Xentorcon assumed Earth's offensive and defensive military capability would not be a problem. Modulated electronic frequencies were mostly in the megahertz band indicating their technology was not advanced."

"The pacification of Reaper #4 will be a takeover, not a battle. What do you recommend for tactics," Xentorcon ask his operations officer?

"I recommend we shock the planet with a global strike using inert kinetic energy weapons. That should produce an immediate surrender with no losses or lasting environmental damage.

If they continue to resist, I'd set up siege units in geo stationary orbit and systematically destroy all major cities, their military, and power generation infrastructure."

"Why so benevolent?"

"We will need the indigenous population to mine ore and grow food. Large scale termination of life is a last resort. If necessary, we should purge one of the major continents of life and prepare it for use as a terrestrial-operations base. That will be the job of our Interceptor squadrons. Once the bases are operational and troops have been landed, pacification of the remainder of the planet will begin."

"Good. Prepare the necessary tactical, communication, weapons and operational orders."

Place: Amyville, Tennessee

Time: 1535 hours, July 10, 2050,

President Nash's declaration of martial law backfired. It convinced people that bad things were about to happen. The country side was invaded by civilians fleeing cities and towns. People, farm animals and pets were being moved into isolated shelters of every imaginable design.

Main streets in towns like Amyville, Tennessee were quiet except for the occasional bark from a lost dog or the sound of wind. Roads were littered with vehicles out of gas or broke down. Personal belongings lay abandoned, too heavy to make the last leg of their owner's journey into the hills. The trail of belongings were like the proverbial bread crumbs, a trail that might lead them back home someday.

The transmission of modulated energy had ceased except for military Broadcasts. People sat, held their loved ones, and listened to civil defense updates on the progress of the aliens.

Place: White House, Washington, DC

*Time: 0835 hours, July 11, 2050

Sally looked at her watch as she walked into the situation room. It was 8:35 AM.

"Good morning."

The watch team was used to her coming in for a quick up date. The senior watch officer was ready for her.

"Good morning Sally. At 1423 hours Greenwich Mean Time, the alien force entered the asteroid field surrounding our solar system. Navigating through the asteroids will slow them down some. The latest estimated time of their arrival is approximately 1100 hours local time today."

"Thanks."

Satisfied, she proceeded to the Oval Office.

"Good morning sir."

"Morning, Sally. I've sent fighters from Grand Forks to Portage. They should be arriving there soon. We'll soon find out what the hell is going on up there."

"What about the chaos in the cities?"

"A few rubber bullets and tear gas will take care of that. Have you had breakfast yet," Nash ask her?

"No, just some coffee."

"Have brunch with me."

"We'll, I have no reason to refuse."

"Good, come with me."

They walked to his private living area. Sally immediately noticed that the table had not been set.

"Where are we going to eat," Sally asked.

"I forgot to tell you, your brunch."

"This is not the time for Nero to play while Rome is burning," she said, lightly tapping his lips with her forefinger.

"I want you."

He turned her around and faced a mirror while he opened up her blouse. Her breasts exposed, he massaged them aggressively.

"Not so ruff," she complained.

He ignored her as he lifted her shirt up around her waist and stripped her panties down like he was peeling a banana. It didn't take long.

"You can clean up in my bathroom. I'll see you in the Oval office when you're done."
"A cold and unfeeling man. There will come a day," she thought with revenge in her heart.

Back in the Oval Office, Nash was busy making phone calls and receiving status reports. Sally walked in.

"You are a son-of-a-bitch," she said.
"Remember our quid pro quo."
"Yes, but in the right proportion, at the right time and the right way."
"I don't have time for proportion."

A call from the White House communication center interrupted them. Nash picked up the phone.

"Yes."
"Mr. President, as you know we've been transmitting your greetings from Earth on multiple frequencies since yesterday. We received a response a few minutes ago.
"Finally, I knew they would want a deal. Read it."
"To the leader of the so called Fourth Realm. I, Xentorcon, leader of the Rendinese Empire, do not negotiate about what I

already have. Your planet, designated Reaper #4, is already a colony in the Rendinese Empire. Do not resist or you will be destroyed. Is there an answer sir?"

Nash was stunned. Were these aliens crazy or just monsters.

"No answer. I can't believe it; they don't even want to hear what I have to say."

"I could have told you that."

"How would you know," Nash asked.

"I know people who know other people. This alien conqueror, Xentorcon, does not negotiate. In a few hours, it is very possible you will be dead. For me, I'm getting out of here and joining my fellow patriots."

"Who do you know, and what can they do that I can't?"

"They are leaders who are loyal to their people and in return get total loyalty back. Something you haven't got. I am a member of the Brothers and Sisters, the BAS. We have been engaged in passive resistance against you for over two years. Since you could be useful in controlling your remaining fanatics, like the Red Staters, you should come with me. At least you'll be alive a while longer."

Place: Portage La Prairie, Manitoba, Canada

Time: 1200 hours, July 11, 2050

It was all hands-on deck at Portage as fighters were refitted with Rendinese weapons. Twenty-two had been refitted at Portage, forty-one at Holberg and thirty-three at Cold Lake. Jeremiah and Miacon were talking in hanger two when they heard the alert sirens go off. Jeremiah grabbed his walkie-talkie.

"Operations, what's going on?"

"In coming planes sir. They identified themselves as Fourth Realm units, so we assumed it wasn't a social call."

"Good call, how many?"

"We've got nine bogies."

"Get fighters in the air now."

"Already happening."

Twelve fighters waiting for refitting took off.

"Scramble Eagles, this is Flight leader, in coming aircraft bearing 195, ten miles. Let's break them up."

At two miles, they over heard a surprise transmission.

"Portage Control. Squawking IFF friendly. Request permission to land."

"Runway two-left, permission to land."

Forty-five minutes later all aircraft were on the ground. The realm squadron leader approached the Portage base commander who was waiting on the tarmac.

They saluted.

"Welcome Commander, why the change of heart?"

"I received a message from Northern Command that the aliens refused Nash's offer to negotiate and he has fled Washington. I decided it was ridiculous for us to try to do to each other what the aliens surely intend to do to all of us."

"Your with us, then?"

"Yes sir, I believe we are."

"Then get in line. Your planes are about to become humanities last line of defense.

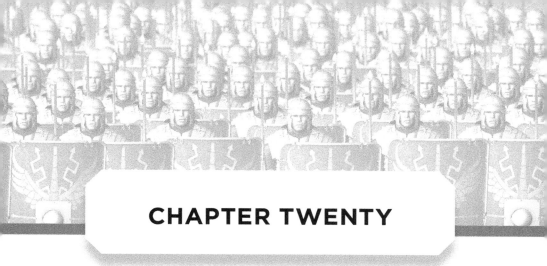

CHAPTER TWENTY

Xentorcon Blitz
Place: Rendinese Armada

Time: 1323 hours, July 11, 2050

WORD SPREAD LIKE WILD fire about the alien's intent, President Nash's disappearance and rumors the BAS were supporting a resistance force in Canada. Red Staters who continued their fanatical activities were now Dead Staters. Loyalist to the Realm were abused, whipped, stripped naked in public and shaved. Nash and Sally fled to Portage La Prairie. Xentorcon, unaware of the chaos on the ground, prepared his forces for action. His advance scouts made visual contact with Earth at 1420 hours.

"Control, this is scout one, no surprises so far. Reaper #4 has one moon and an amazing amount of junk in low to medium orbit."

On board Xentorcon's battle cruiser pilots sat in their fighters nervously listening to the tactical communications circuit. The signal to launch was given by Command control on Xentorcon's Battle Cruiser. Once in the air, squadron leaders took over.

"All units, this is Empire 0ne, proceed to your final weapons launch positions and prepare for simultaneous release of munitions. After the strike is complete, all units return to your base ship."

"Base Control, this is Empire One. Interceptors on station."

"Release."

Place: Amyville, Tennessee

Time: 1340 hours, July 11, 2050

On the ground, thousands of hypervelocity impacts destroyed an eclectic array of large and small buildings, power plants, planes, airports, residential areas, ships and equipment of all sorts. Power grids and communications networks were down all over the world. Targeting of kinetic energy masses concentrated on highly illuminated areas. Southern Mexico, most of Canada, the Amazon region of South America, the Steppes in Russia and Northern Africa received little attention.

From the mountains and foot hills surrounding Los Angeles, Denver, Tokyo, London and hundreds of other cities, residents watched in horror as the destruction rained down.

At an average impact velocity of ten thousand feet per second, anyone near the impact point and less than a couple hundred feet underground was doomed. The Earth looked as if it had a horrible case of burning, smoking acne.

People in Amyville could see the plasma trails created by the kinetic masses as they streaked to the ground in places like Knoxville and Memphis. Like meteors, the atmospheric ablation of their heat shields glowed white. At 10,000 feet per second, they hit the ground before you could hear them.

In Amyville, one body impacted in a shopping mall parking lot creating a crater large enough to contain several school buses. Two more impacted outside of town causing little damage. The only thing people could do was hold each other and pray.

Place: Portage, Manitoba, Canada

Time: 1440 hours, July 11, 2050

Jeremiah and Miacon stood in the air operations center listening to encrypted military transmissions. They assumed the barrage of kinetic weapons would be followed by a conbined air and land attack. They decided to commit.

"Commander, launch aircraft immediately. Send them out on southern vectors, ten degree apart. At least we'll be in the air when they come."

"Will do."

"And Commander, wish them God speed."

"Colonel, just received a report that very large blips have been detected by a radar system called 'Space Fence'. It's an S-band radar designed for tracking space debris."

"That would be Xentorcon's battle cruisers. They are the mother ships for his interceptors and invasion troops," Miacon said.

"Did they give a position?"

"Yes sir, equatorial geostationary orbit, spaced evenly around the globe."

"Give Warren AFB the coordinates and tell them to launch when ready."

"Yes sir."

Twenty minutes later, the flash from the Exo-atmospheric detonations of nuclear weapons could be seen in the sky. Like mini supernovas, they created a burst of light sufficient to turn night into day for a few seconds.

"Damn, they worked," Mary said.

The nuclear warheads worked but did not disable the cruisers. But the Electromagnetic pulse created by the detonations made the Global Positioning System (GPS) and communication satellites useless.

*Place: North Dakota Air space *

Time: 1516 hours, July 11, 2050

20,000 feet over North Dakota and Minnesota, the refitted fighters, renamed the BAS squadrons, could see the rain of kinetic energy from space. Then it stopped.

"Flight leader, Mustang I, the barrage appears to be over, they'll becoming soon."
"Mustang I, concur, all units, conduct weapon and targeting system checks. Prepare to engage."

The interceptor's small radar cross section allowed them to get close to the fighters without detection. At five miles distance, Flight Leader could see them visually.

"Flight Leader, Red Dog, I have a visual, One o'clock, estimate 35,000 feet."
"This is Flight leader. All units engage at will."

Shortly after Red Dog completed his transmission, the temperature of his cockpit started to rise.

"Flight leader, Red Dog, the heat, why is it so hot?"

She was sweating profusely and having trouble breathing.

"Red Dog your being lased. Roll out, take evasive action."

She fired two fusion torpedoes then rotated her shoulders counter clock wise and tilted her head left while increasing engine thrust to 90 percent. The ergonomic sensors in her cockpit responded immediately, she could feel her g suit squeezing her legs. She accelerated out of the laser beam then completed a reverse up and over helical maneuver that placed her behind the less maneuverable interceptor.

Before she could react, she found herself in a continuous wave laser beam. She managed to get a three second burst with her 25-millimeter cannon before disappearing in a ball of exploding gas, fire and debris.

One of Red Dog's torpedoes hit the interceptor. It began to yaw, then slowly rolled clock wise. Mustang I saw numerous Rendinese bail out as Earth's gravity took over and pulled the interceptor down. It became just another kinetic energy impact in a corn field.

World-wide, Xentorcon's interceptors destroyed over 9,000 war planes. The BAS squadron destroyed 17 interceptors while suffering a 95% loss rate. At 0515 EST it was over. The first wave of Rendinese troops began to land around globe. The troopers used gyroscopically stabilized assault weapons that made every trooper a marksman. With interceptors providing ground support with fusion bombs and high energy particle beam weapons, Earth didn't have a chance.

Major Hunt braced for the worst but no one showed up. Xentorcon's ground forces first priority was major population areas. He would clean up peripheral areas like Thompson in phase two.

"Xentorcon, Reaper #4's air power has been completely neutralized. Our losses were minimal. 17 were destroyed by their own weapons."

"That's impossible, they all have launch ship avoidance blocks in their guidance software. Which squadrons had this problem?

"That's strange, it was only squadron five."

"Where were they deployed?"

"West of the big lakes, about 46 degrees above the planets equator. In this region," he replied circling North Dakota and Minnesota.

"Has Miacon or any of his ships been found yet?"

"No."

"Well, I smell a river lizard. Miacon has not shown up, but I think his weapons did. They were fixed to Reaper #4 fighters. That is the only explanation. Our weapons cannot strike their own launch platforms. I want interceptors and troops sent to all landing fields capable of supporting fighters within 500 quartiles of the center of squadron five's patrol area."

"Acknowledged, Xentorcon."

Place: Portage La Prairie, Manitoba, Canada

Time: 1600 hours, July 11, 2050

Jeremiah, President Nash, Sally, Mary, Miacon and Tacon sat at a table in Air Operations lamenting the inevitability of the situation. Nash's two security guards stayed outside nervously watching for trouble.

"The situation is grim. We have no effective defense against Xentorcon. It will only be a matter of time until troops show up. Hiding in the woods will work for a short time. If anything happens, an injury, sickness or being tracked down and shot, hiding is not a long-term option."

"We need to consider surrendering, if we want a chance to survive," Nash said.

Mary stood up and faced President Nash. She surprised everyone by slapping him in the face. He resisted the urge to punch her.

"That's something coming from you. You're as bad as Xentorcon."

"You can hate me, but it changes nothing. We have to deal with the world as it is, not as we want it to be," Nash said.

"Miacon, our only hope for the future is you. Before we surrender, you must return to Xylanthia and seek assistance for Earth," Jeremiah said.

"I agree, but getting away undetected will be difficult."

"Use one Interceptor, squawk Rendinese military codes, maintain full stealth and electronic silence. Send two of your interceptors to LEO broadcasting surrender signals. In the confusion, you may be able to slip away. Leave on a polar cap trajectory and go to light speed as soon as you're out of the sensible atmosphere."

"That means I won't have time to send out path clearance probes. I guess it is the only way."

"We have no choice; I wish you luck."

"Let my ships at Holberg and Cold Lake know what is going on."

By 1725 hours, Miacon was off the planet and heading for Xylanthia. It was just in time because Xentorcon's forces showed up at 1830 hours. Jeremiah told everyone not to resist. Fighting to the death would serve no purpose at this point. Everyone stood grimly watching troopers march onto the airbase. Jeremiah and his team were standing outside of hanger two, waiting. A ground transporter drove up to them and stopped. An officer got out and approached them.

"I represent the Rendinese Empire. This facility is now under our control. If you resist, you will be destroyed."

Only Tacon understood Rendinese, so he replied.

"We will offer no resistance."

"You speak Rendinese. Who are you?"

"I am Tacon from Earth."

"You don't look like the others."

"I was born on Earth to a human father and Rendinese mother."

"Which makes you neither. I want to know where a Rendinese named Miacon is?"

"I won't lie. He was here, but has fled the planet."

"Tell him who I am, and that Earth surrenders," Nash said.

"The leader of North America has instructed me to tell Xentorcon we surrender."

"What about the rest of the planet?"

"When they hear President Nash has surrendered, they will do the same."

"Acknowledged, I will convey your message to Xentorcon."

CHAPTER TWENTY-ONE

Quiet Desperation
Place: Missile Site, Manitoba, Canada

Time: 0900 July 24, 2050

XENTORCON HONORED THE TERMS of Earth's surrender in principal only. No mass destruction of Earth or genocide in return for unconditional surrender, but he systematically destroyed the world's military infrastructure and turned several bases into concentration camps for anyone foolish enough to put up resistance.

North America was divided into Pacification Zones that were sized according to the population density in the area. The pacification process was simple. Troopers assembled at various points along the border of each zone at 4:00 AM EST on July 5, forming irregular circles around each zone. At dawn they began shrinking the radius of the circle, forcing people into a tighter and tighter group near the center.

Amyville, Tennessee was in the center of one of the zones. Sunday mornings are always quiet in Amyville. This particular morning, there was absolute silence. The town was mostly empty except for a few people who had decided that fleeing was futile. They would accept whatever fate the aliens had in store for them.

This Sunday morning would be like no other. Citizens woke up to the sound of troopers shouting orders in Rendinese that no one understood. The troopers got their message across with hand gestures, head nods and dead blow blunt force wands that could break bones. Once everyone was rounded up, an officer who had attended the Rendinese language school and spoke basic English, addressed them.

"Orders from Xentorcon, leader of the Rendinese Empire's occupation of Reaper #4, are as follows:

1. A curfew exists between 2300 hours and 0600 hours local time.
2. Weapons and ammunition must be turned in immediately.
3. Orders given by any Rendinese are to be strictly obeyed.
4. Resistance will result in immediate arrest and movement to a concentration camp.
5. No one is permitted to leave the zone.

The orders were amazingly similar to President Nash's standing orders. Dictators think the same way.

After the orders were read, a senior trooper stepped forward; he stood staring at the crowd of town's people. His small dark eyes had the look of someone accustomed to command.

He was Ramacon, the egocentric but capable leader and principal deputy to Emperor Xentorcon. He would not normally participate in pacification operations, but wanted a dozen or so humans for interrogation. He would select a male and a female from Amyville. His philosophy was that in order to effectively control intelligent life forms, their psychology and manner of thinking must be understood.

He was a little worried about how easy the pacification process had been so far. Amyville was especially easy by Rendinese standards. Those that did fight back were mostly civilians shooting from the woods or setting booby traps. He was also amazed that the indigenous people of Reaper #4, though generally smaller in stature, were similar to his people in many ways. The males were weaker but some of the women would be acceptable temporary substitutes for Rendinese females.

"This is turning out to be a strange place, I must be careful," he thought.

"Have the squad leaders report to me in one-hour Reaper #4 time. I will set up in that building over there," he said, pointing to a building across the street.

"The one marked 'April's Bakery'?"

"Yes, and have my things brought in."

He also did not trust Reaper #4's leadership. Their pitiful defense and quick surrender made no sense to him. Rendinese leaders at any level, would only surrender if faced with certain death. If there was some kind of plan in the works, he would find out soon.

"Somebody here is going to tell me if something clever is going on or I will make them wish they had died at the beginning of the invasion," Ramacon thought.

Ramacon walked into the Bakery twenty minutes later. He stood at the entrance scanning the interior. He could not figure out what type of place it was. There were a couple small tables with chairs and a long counter. There was a strange smell. He gazed at the half dozen people standing in the corner who were quietly staring back at him. He walked up to one of the females and eyed her up and down.

"What is this place, a meeting center, and what is that smell?" The young female stood paralyzed with fear, unable to answer.

"This is a bakery." One of the men answered.

"What is a bakery and what the River Lizard is that smell," he demanded.

"This place makes food and the smell is coming from the food we serve," a man said while making a gesture of putting food in his mouth.

"It is disgusting. All of you sit down," he ordered, pointing to the tables.

"I will be using this building as a base for the night. Any trouble, discipline will be harsh and immediate."

Just then his aide walked in with his personal bags. A few minutes later his squad leaders arrived.

"Let's use the center table. Everyone take a seat."

"Would you like a drink sir?" one of the women asked.

"We have our own fluids."

"The bottles behind the counter are what people use to relax. It's called hard Cider and makes you feel good without impairing you in any way," she offered.

It was a small lie. They thought that if they could get the invaders drunk, maybe they would be able to get an advantage over them. Ramacon told one of his squad leaders to check out the bottles.

"Can one of you prepare food?"

"All of us can," one of the women answered.

"Take the young female with the light hair to the back of the restaurant where they prepare their food and instruct her how to prepare our rations. Don't take your eyes of her for a minute."

"Ramacon, I tested the bottled liquid with my field analyzer. I think they are telling the truth. They are mostly a mix of water, flavoring and intoxicant," one of his soldiers reported with a very satisfied look on his face.

"Very well, bring a few containers to the table."

In the mean-time a squad leader went to the kitchen with the young waitress and unpacked the bag of rations. He began to instruct her on the process of preparing the food. As he read each step, he began to notice that her body wasn't very different from Rendinese females. A little short maybe but he could smell her from six feet away. A good smell, but he was not used to people with such strong odors. Altogether, he concluded she was quite acceptable.

Just then she bent over to get a skillet out of one of the lower drawers. As she bent over, he caught a quick view of the top of her breasts. He became distracted as he focused more on her than the rations. He reached around her and began to fondle her breasts.

"Stop it, please stop it," she begged as she struggled to get away.

"I want to see your body."

"Are you crazy, I want out of here," she begged again.

"If you take your cloths of and give me just a few minutes, I will not tell anyone and we will not kill your friends when we leave," a promise he could not guarantee but he hoped it would scare her enough to get her to comply with his wishes.

"Please don't hurt me or my friends."

"I will not hurt you, just stop fighting and do as I say."

She took all of her clothes off and stood in front of him almost weeping with embarrassment. He had her fondle him for a minute as he caressed her breasts. The rest only took a minute.

"Get dressed and finish the rations," he ordered.

"How can you be so mechanical and degrading," she asked.

"I needed you and besides you're an alien prisoner," he rationalized to himself.

"You are just a thing to me. I cannot care about someone or a people that I may have to kill."

The squad leader came from a good family and was not particularly proud of what he had just done, but he could not let himself care. They finished up and brought the rations to Ramacon's table.

"Sit down and have a drink squad leader. It is pretty good stuff. You were in the food heating area quite a while. I can tell by the look on her face, that you did more than prepare rations. Tell me, what does she fell like?" Ramacon ask.

"We only prepared rations."

"Whatever you say, but I might just have to take one of these females and do my own research. Now that we are all together, I want everyone to set their time to Reaper #4 time. We going to be on this planet for a while. Tomorrow we will meet up with four additional squads, I'll leave one squad here, and move on to the next town. In addition to our pacification objective, I want to find out if the humans have a plan of some sort that could threaten us, so keep you eyes and ears open. Send the three males to their homes; I am taking one of the females for the night. The rest of you can fight over the other two."

The squad leader who had used the young female in the kitchen immediately jumped up and grabbed her again.

"This one's mine," he declared.

As the troopers went off to find shelter for the night, the men in the bakery lamented that their strategy to get the aliens drunk and then escape had failed. The next morning, Ramacon and his men assembled in the square outside of the Bakery.

"We are missing one squad leader."

"He probably stayed up half the night playing with that alien female and getting intoxicated," Ramacon said.

"Get the first squad into their vehicles and find the squad leader now," Ramacon ordered with irritation in his voice.

The squad leader was in a panic as he fumbled to get into his uniform and collect his gear. The young waitress sat on a chair with a blanket around her. She had convinced him to shelter in her house. The presence of her mother and maybe a neighbor, might help her deal with her captor. It didn't help much.

The alien soldier had forced himself on her for sure, but he was not mean, nor did he hurt her. It was not the physical sex per say, she had been with men before. It was that he had not ask, he had not courted her, he just took her. Sex is offensive when it's stolen. He started to walk toward the door then suddenly stopped. He had heard what sounded like radio static and a human communicating on a transceiver of some sort. He said nothings and turned to face her.

"What is your name?"

"April," she responded, surprised that he asked.

"I am not proud of yesterday. I am sure you hate me and would kill me if you could. I won't bother you again."

"Squad Leader," someone outside the building yelled.

185

"Coming," he yelled as he ran out of the building.

"Good thing we found you. If you had missed departure this morning, Ramacon would have had you whipped."

"I know, I know. Listen, I'm not sure, but I think someone in the basement of this house is using a communication device."

They turned on a frequency analyzer.

"You are right. Estimate 300-watt, 60 Mega-hertz source; inside the home."

They searched the house and found a woman sitting in front of a transmitter control unit. April had followed them down to the basement.

"She's my mother, please don't hurt her," April begged.

"No one is going to get hurt if you cooperate. Who were you talking to?"

"It's just a hobby, something I do for fun," she replied.

"What are these notes. I warn you; I have been trained in your language."

"It's how I keep track of things, it's my log."

"Who is BAS?"

"My friend in Memphis."

"What's his full name?"

"Bob Steele," she said making things up and beginning to sweat.

"You are lying. You report Rendinese troop movements for the fun of it?"

"It's the only thing that's going on, so we talk about it." She knew she was caught in a lie.

"You are under arrest. There will be a guard posted outside, so don't try anything. Seize the communicator."

They reported the incident to Ramacon.

"The letters BAS appears numerous times in these notes. The old woman was sending position reports and trooper movements to whoever the BAS is."

"Keep her confined for now. Knoxville is a big town. I'll collect a dozen people, and we will find out who the BAS is. Squad #1 is in charge.

CHAPTER TWENTY-TWO

With an Iron Fist
Place: Knoxville, Tennessee

Time: 10:35 hours, July 25, 2050

THE TRANSIT TO KNOXVILLE was uneventful except for the stifling heat and humidity. Mosquitoes and Saddleback Moths tortured Ramacon's troopers at night and the lack of air-conditioning in their tactical transporters added to the misery.

When they entered Knoxville, Ramacon dispersed his troopers through out the town. Most headed for air-conditioned buildings. The two things they liked about Earth was coffee and air-conditioning in every building. People readily directed him to the town's leader, Mayor Swinton.

"I am Ramacon, temporary commander of this continent, I represent Emperor Xentorcon."

"We can sit at the conference table and discuss...."

"Have them stripped and tied to chairs," Ramacon ordered before the Mayor could finish.

"What are your plans for the defense of this planet," Ramacon demanded? No one spoke.

Ramacon pulled a hand held weapon out of its holster, dialed in stun and zapped one of the Mayor's staff in the foot. It left a serious burn and made the officer yell out in pain.

"What have you instructed the general population to do?" No one spoke.

He zapped the same staff man on his testicles, burning half the skin off. This time the man not only screamed, he urinated on himself and the chair. He then passed out. Ramacon turned to Swinton.

"I am going to start over on another man with the same questions and continue until you are the only one left. I promise you, that if it gets that far, you will beg for death."

Swinton gave in.

"Don't torture anyone else; I'll answer your questions."

"What are your plans for the defense of this planet?"

"We have surrendered, there is no defense. We have no more deployed nuclear weapons; all of our fighter aircraft were destroyed in your attack."

"What have you instructed the general population to do?"

"Basically, disperse to the country as we assumed the cities were going to be targeted. we don't have the capability to fight you. I'm just a small town leader, I don't tell the people what to do."

Ramacon contemplated his answer.

"You tried to surprise us in low orbit. I am still suspicious of your intent. If you are lying, I will punish thousands of your people.

Do you understand," He ask as he jerked Swinton's head back by
his hair.

"Yes, Yes."

"Good, now who is BAS?"

Swinton looked at his friend lying on the floor. He decided to
tell a half truth.

"They are Earth's information network. Regular government
and commercial news broadcasts are not available. The BAS has
no weapons and they're all civilian amateurs."

"But they are capable of sharing information about troop
movements and encouraging passive resistance. You will make a
communication announcing you have surrendered the city and
no further resistance will be tolerated. Tell your city the alien
commander has said he will kill one hundred people for every
vehicle or soldier harmed. Do it."

He untied the Mayor but left the others in their chairs. Swinton
was pleased Knoxville would not be destroyed. After he called the
local radio station and dictated his message, Ramacon brought him
back into the conference room.

"Destroy them and return to your vehicles," Ramacon ordered.

"Why," Swinton begged.

He barely got the question out of his mouth, before the high
energy lasers burned him and his staff. Ramacon then walked
outside and yelled for the leader of squad #3 to come forward.

"I am leaving your squad here for the time being. I want
the Amyville BAS communication apparatus left on and
monitored. These humans are up to something, I am sure of it.

Any communication you hear, forward it to me immediately. any questions?"

"None Ramacon," the squad leader replied with a simultaneous salute and hand slap to his left hip.

He stood and watched until Ramacon and his troops were out of sight. He then gathered his unit around him to shared his commander's orders.

"Ramacon has left me in charge of this city and the surrounding area until further ordered. Squad #1 is monitoring Amyville BAS communications and we will remain here to keep a close watch on the local population. I want a three-circle integrated and networked sensor field. Set up the inner circle around the Mayor's office complex, the second one at a diameter of five pentians and an outer circle big enough to encompass the city.

I want the local BAS transmitter found. Set up our communication and sensor monitoring station in the Mayor's office.

"Where should we stay?"

"The Mayor's office complex. Break into two-man teams and chose a room. We will begin patrolling the sensor areas by quadrant and make a daily report to Ramacon, questions?"

"What about the local population. They are not as I imagined, you know, they look somewhat like us, and some of the females are, well, let's say, easy to look at." A few chuckles emanated from the men.

"It will get lonely here pretty fast."

"On your own time, I don't care what you do."

Place: Jason's Shopping Mall, Knoxville, Tenn.

*Time: 0800 hours EST, July 26, 2050

The citizens that remained in Knoxville watched as the aliens patrolled the streets. Always in two-man teams. They never engaged in personal interactions, they just starred at people as they went by. At 0800 hours on July 26, two alien troopers entered a shopping Mall in Knoxville's North end.

The Mall was not open, but there were humans inside cleaning, working inventory and preparing food for sale when the Mall opened. Half the stores were boarded up.

The troopers slowly headed to the food court in the middle of the Mall. As they went by, people looked at them with their periphery vision, not wanting to make direct eye contact.

"I don't know how these humans eat what they eat. It smells like rotting lizards."

"What they drink isn't bad though. The coffee we had last night was okay."

Neither of the troopers were fluent in English, but one of them had picked up some key words. They approached an area where they thought they were smelling coffee. A young woman stood behind a counter looking at them. The troopers approached her.

"Coffee?"

"Cream and sugar," she asked.

"No English," was the response.

She added cream and sugar and handed the coffees to the troopers. They both took a good drink and immediately spit it out.

The coffee was too hot and burned their mouths. They assumed the woman had done it on purpose and were angry. They came around the counter and grabbed her by the wrist spewing angry words in Rendinese. A young man in the back came out and tried to punch one of the troopers.

"Get off her, assholes," he said loudly.

The troopers were just to strong. They twisted the man's arm until it snapped and threw him over the counter onto the floor. He laid there moaning. People saw what was happening but were initially afraid to interfere. The troopers pointed their weapons at the crowd and fired. Five people were wounded or fell dead. The rest ran away screaming except for a woman who dropped to her knees, frozen by fear.

One of the troopers grabbed her and they took both woman into the back of the store. They used their standard issue wrist restraints to secure them to stainless steel tables and promptly removed their clothing.

Before they could pleasure themselves, a dozen men barged in completely surprising the troopers. Four of the men had pistols. The trooper closest to them was struck by four shots in the chest and abdomen. The second trooper started firing his energy weapon but one of the men put a round into his leg. The impact of the bullet distracted him just enough to allow four of the men to grad a hold of him.

Even wounded, the trooper was formidable and threw the men off him. In the confusion of the altercation a fifth man put two more rounds into troopers. It was over. They released the woman and told them to get dressed.

"There will be hell to pay now," one of the men said.

"I know, we've got to get rid of these bodies and clean up the place. I suggest we put the aliens in my Van and park it along the river. We'll set fire to it."

"That's a little extreme?"

"Remember the announcement. 100 of us for every trooper harmed or attacked. We're talking about 400 people."

"I hear you, let's get moving."

The incident at Jason's Mall was one of many around the country. The BAS circuits were reporting hundreds of executions in places like Los Angles, Chicago, New York, Quebec, Mexico City and many other cities. Jeremiah and Tacon listened and waited in Portage La Prairie, praying for a miracle.

Place: Concentration Camp, Millington, Tenn.

Time: 10:00 hours EST, July 26, 2050

Pacification zones were designed to control the general population within their existing living and working environment. As long as you obeyed the rules, you were mostly free to go about things as usual. The unfortunate people who provoked the Rendinese in some way ended up in places like the old Naval Support Activity in Millington, Tennessee, just north of Memphis, where life was as boring as it was frightening.

The Rendinese version of a concentration camp was draconian but not life threatening. It was more like the Japanese-American Internment Camps used during WW II than a Nazi concentration camp. Prisoners were awoken at dawn, got dressed, made their beds, rushed to the wash building to wipe off with a wash rag, defecate if they could, constipation meant you lived with it for the rest of the day because being late for roll call was the first opportunity to get a whack across the back with a baton.

Breakfast was sufficient but very limited in variety and was usually oatmeal without milk or sugar and black coffee. The Rendinese had asked human cooks what food item they could prepare in bulk and people would be able to eat it every day for a month. Oat meal made the final cut for breakfast. Broth with bread for lunch and boiled root vegetables for dinner. The only seasonings were salt and pepper. The coffee was good because the Rendinese liked it as well.

Work assignments were sporadic and unscheduled. Whatever the work was, it is always with your hands, rags or small plastic hand held gardening tools. The Rendinese would not put metal tools in to the hands of prisoners. The work is sometimes hard, like digging a new latrine, boring, like cleaning and scrubbing, or trivial, like picking up small rocks and pebbles from the camp grounds. Free time was spent milling about the grounds, walking and talking.

A siren signals evening roll call. Prisoners are lined up by rows of twenty. The Troopers then check the tag around each prisoner's neck and enters it into an electronic log. To the prisoners roll call served no useful purpose other than to harass them. No one ever tried to escape. The sentences were one to three months, the camp was not life threatening and beatings had to be earned. There was nowhere to escape to anyhow. The Rendinese had cleverly set up interment within a zone, a camp within a camp.

CHAPTER TWENTY-THREE

Miacon Returns
*Place: Planet Xylanthia,
Sirius Solar System*

*Time: 1320 hours EST, August 4, 2050

MIACON STARED AT THE visual on his tactical display. Xylanthia was the size of an apple and getting bigger. Soon he would be home. He had many silent supporters and with Xentorcon away pacifying Earth, he was also hopping for a miracle. He decided to go in the front door.

"Central Control, this is Miacon. Request landing instructions."
"Miacon, what are your intentions?"
"To return home and help my people."
"Standby, escort interceptors are being dispatched."

Miacon saw the Battle Cruisers positioned in low orbit. He assumed they were watching his every move.
Interceptors arrived within minutes.

"Miacon, this is vector control. You are instructed to follow me to Xylanthia Air Field six."

"Understand, maneuvering to stations now."

On the ground, there was no celebratory greeting nor was he arrested.

"I have been instructed to take you to Besicon's office immediately upon landing."

"Who is Besicon?"

"She is Xentorcon's political second and in temporary command while he is away."

Upon arriving at command headquarters, they were immediately escorted into Besicon's office. Miacon was stunned.

"Lava, I never expected to find you working here. You were always a country person. Where is your boss?"

Miacon assumed his old girlfriend was an aide or administrative person of some kind.

"I am Besicon, Emperor Xentorcon's second in command. He thought Lava was too female sounding for my position and ask me to change my name."

"It's still a shock."

"I wish to speak with Miacon alone."

Everyone vacated. Besicon and Miacon sat down at a table with Pulp Tea and sweets.

"Where have you been and more importantly, why are you back?"

"I know I must be unpopular to many Rendinese but I did not like the direction Xentorcon was taking us. An Empire based on personal loyalty to a dictator leads to a two-class society. I did what I did as a patriot, not a traitor."

"Xentorcon will never appreciate or accept that point of view."

"I agree. I came back for two reasons. One, I'm tired of being a fugitive and two, I intend to convince my people there is a better way. I'm going to remind them of what it was like before our universe collapsed. We were a strong but peace-loving Empire. If Xentorcon is allowed to continue his Reaper strategy, we will rot from the inside out and be hated by all intelligent life in this sector of the galaxy."

Besicon looked at him but did not respond. She picked up her communicator and called someone whose name Miacon didn't recognize.

"I should consider you a threat. But let us finish our tea. There are two people I want you to meet. While we are waiting, tell me what your life has been like since we last met."

"Not much to tell, you remember I left for the Fleet Academy after we broke up. I graduated fourth in my class and scored 100% on the light speed navigation exam. Based on my performance, I was assigned as assistant navigator on Battle Cruiser RE-04. The next fifteen years I assumed positions of increasing responsibility, ending up head of the Rendinese Space Fleet. You know the rest."

"You never mated?"

"I had a few friends over the years, but no, I never mated. It is hard to be committed to someone in my profession. What about you?"

"After you left, I went to school for Politics and Government Administration. Before our universe collapsed, I was a speech writer for the Rendinese government leader at the time. After, the great migration to Xylanthia, Xentorcon noticed me. I guess he liked the way a I looked."

"Did you mate?"

"No. But we had a relationship with an unspoken quid pro quo. He mentored me and gave me great responsibility in return for satisfying his needs. The only wonderful thing that came out of our relationship was my daughter."

"She would probably be grown by now."

"Yes, and she is beautiful."

Three senior military officers appeared at the entrance to Besicon's office.

"Besicon, you ask to see us?"

"Yes, please come in and have a seat."

Besicon introduced the three males as head of the Space Fleet, Trooper Corps and Xentorcon's Industrial Cartel. All three recognized Miacon.

"Besicon, no constraints?"

"I have known Miacon my entire life. He poses no physical threat.

Besicon pointed her communicator at a black box mounted near the entrance to her office. The sound of security locks engaging, windows turning opaque and a white noise playing in the background could be heard.

"This space is now set for Xentorcon level I discussions. No one will know what we are going to talk about."

"Your trust in Miacon is breathtaking."

"I am convinced he is a patriot who can be trusted. Miacon, there are many among us who are disgusted with Xentorcon's methods. He is a dangerous and powerful leader who maintains loyalty through enabling the worse in people. Greed, lust for power and protection from accountability, no matter what they do. We are the silent resistance."

"This is the miracle I was hoping for. I am with you completely. Do you have a plan?"

"We do, but we need a strong, capable leader. None of us can lead a Space Fleet Armada in battle. We are staff officer's expert in strategic, logistics and operational planning."

Everyone stared at Miacon.

"And you think that is me."

"We know you can do it."

"Again, what is your plan?"

"We know who is loyal and who is going through the motions to avoid trouble for themselves and their families. We are going to put an operational plan together for a Reaper #5 mission.

We will ensure the Battle Cruisers, Interceptors and auxiliary ships for that mission will be led and manned by Xentorcon loyalist. They will be told the rest of the fleet will remain as a home guard while they are away. Once they are deployed, you will take command of the home guard, deploy to Earth and engage Xentorcon. When you return, you will be the leader of the Rendinese people."

"I like your plan. You know what will happen if I fail?"

"Yes, we know, but the alternative is just as frightening. Xentorcon has eyes for my young daughter. If we fail, I will be forced to kill him myself," Besicon said.

They all stood up and faced each other in a circle.

"May the spirits and the honor of the Rendinese people be with you, Miacon," Besicon said.

Place: Fort Thompson, Manitoba, Canada

Time: 0430 hours, August 11, 2050

Major hunt sat on the roof of his quarters scanning the night sky. He wondered about many things. Why hadn't the aliens attacked his base and why hasn't Miacon returned. Morale was low. They had been on alert for a long time. His soldiers missed their families and Thompson was nearly empty. Many people had fled to higher latitudes, so female companionship was difficult to find. His soldiers were drinking too much and three female soldiers were pregnant. He thoughts were interrupted by a Sargent.

"Major, you need to come and listen to the Ham radio traffic."

Huddled around the Ham Radio, they listened to sound of hope.

"This is BAS Quebec; BAS Washington is reporting a large alien forces approaching Earth. Word is Xentorcon's sensors are tracking it and he is repositioning his forces for some reason. Amateur astronomers have confirmed the presence of the new alien force."

"The question is, are they Xentorcon's reinforcements or Miacon bringing the miracle we have been praying for? Check with Portage and find out what Colonel Astor knows? Keep monitoring the BAS traffic," Major Hunt ordered.

The answer to Hunt's question soon revealed itself. BAS traffic began reporting significant troop movements. The Rendinese were abandoning small towns and setting up defensive positions that included surface-to-air weapons. Deep space probe signals from a loyalist on Xylanthia indicated Miacon was in hot pursuit with the Rendinese home guard. Xentorcon positioned half of his fleet in geostationary orbit 180 degrees away from Miacon's approach vector. The rest of the fleet prepared for direct conflict.

Place: Miacon's Armada, Earth's Solar System

Time: 0915 hours EST, August 11, 2050

Miacon was less than 200-million kilometers away, about two-thirds of the distance between Earth and Mars, and anticipating the coming action. He knew Xentorcon would have discovered his presence by now and would be ready for action.

He decided to split his armada into three attack forces designated as the Gold, Blue and Green Battle Groups. Gold would conduct a direct frontal attack while Blue and Green forces would engage from the left and right flanks.

"Miacon, we have just passed the twenty-million-kilometer point. Recommend slowing to planetoid approach speed."

"Do it. Go to zero closure rate at 500,000 kilometers. Have we detected any enemy ships?"

"Yes, and their message signals."

Crews were a buzz with activity. Final engagement orders were transmitted.

"All units, this is Miacon. Xentorcon has a militarily superior force. He will have more Battle Cruisers than we have. Victory will require an above and beyond effort. Blue and Green Battle groups are currently being given vectors to their area of responsibility. May the spirits be with us. Miacon out."

Miacon sat listening to probe recordings. Interceptors were being launched on all vectors. He knew Xentorcon's fleet was there, he just couldn't see them visually yet. His shipboard sensors operated at the speed of light only and they had no long-distance telescopes, but super-light speed probes were bringing back Xentorcon's message traffic. Interceptor scouts RI-121, 145 and 163 were dispatched towards Earth.

"This is Scout Leader, you know our orders, take station on my port and starboard sides at one-kilometer distance. Tighten it up 145,".

"Give someone their first flight leader assignment and it goes to their head.

"Very funny, 163, just keep it tight. You'll get your ego trip soon enough."

Place: Xentorcon's Battle Cruiser, Earth's Solar System

Time: 1015 hours EST, August 11, 2050

Xentorcon positioned his ships in geostationary orbit as planned and stood in front of his control bridge tactical display reviewing probe data. 'Geo' avoided Low Earth Orbit, what is referred to as 'LEO', where two Space Stations and over 800 satellites shared space with 20,000 trackable pieces of junk.

"All units, if and when necessary, entering Earth's atmosphere is to be confined to the North and South Poles. We must minimize the risk posed by clutter in low Earth orbit."

At 1029 hours EST, Miacon's battle groups came within visual range.

"All units, this is Control, engage at will.

Just then, RN-87, transporting Ramacon to Xentorcon's Battle Cruiser, reported he had been hit by a piece of space debris.

"Control, 87, Flight Computer system off line and hull integrity lost. Losing attitude."

RN-87 began to roll. The resulting centrifugal force caused severed cables and escaping gases to spew outward in all directions. When it entered Earth's atmosphere it exploded.

"Did you see that explosion?"
"I think it was one of our ships but there were no enemy forces at that altitude, they must have had some kind of accident," The trooper assumed.
"It must have self-destructed for some reason."

Xentorcon would not realize until after the battle that his friend and second in command, had perished in the accident.

Place: Earth and Near-Earth Space

Time: 1112 hours EST, August 11, 2050

Both fleets were launching Interceptors. Soon, over 450 ships converged at an average altitude of one-million Kilometers. To an observer on the Moon, Earth looked like an agitated Bee hive. The next two hours were controlled chaos

"I'm on fire, ejecting now."
"My missiles hit but had no effect. I'm...,"

Interceptors from both fleets exploded and descended to Earth's surface, a cluster of smoking, burning pieces. People on the ground watched dozens of interceptors impact the ground, their smoke trails soon becoming zig zag patterns as atmospheric shear wins redesigned them.

"You are being lased, roll out, roll out."

Before the pilot could respond, his ship blew up. In the Green Battle Group area, RN-96 was using a high energy laser and a neutral particle beam to engage and destroy several Interceptors at once. Unlike fixed guns on Earth's military fighters, energy beam weapons could be trained to a different target almost instantly without maneuvering the ship. Suddenly his weapons control computer locked up.

"Battle Control, I need to break off," A Xentorcon pilot yelled into his communicator.
"You will remain engaged," was the answer.
"77, bogie at two o'clock."
"I see it, weapon's loop closed, firing."

One of Miacon's Interceptors, RN-18, soon began to heat up as a high energy microwave laser excited the molecules in its hull. Chemical and oxygen tanks began to explode, he disengaged and headed for his mother ship.

All Rendinese ships are true space ships. In the vacuum of space, there is no atmospheric drag. Therefore, much of the piping, electrical conduits, hydraulic lines and chemical tanks are mounted externally, maximizing interior space. They have some protective armor but cannot handle a direct hit.

The aggressive commander of the Blue Battle Group bombarded Xentorcon's left flank Battle Cruiser with everything it had. Beam weapons created hot spots on its hull and two burner torpedoes hit, but ran out of fuel before they could burn through its thick hull. Like knats buzzing around an over ripe watermelon, Interceptors were everywhere. RN-57 was heading for a Battle Cruiser's vulnerable Ion Engine nozzles.

"Control, this is RN-57, significant damage to exterior hull structure. Weapons control Conduits have been severed and external chemical and fuel tanks are burning. Disengaging to extinguish fires."

At the same time RN-212 was attacking Miacon's Cruiser. The pilot managed to put a burner torpedo on a thinner area of the hull, near a landing dock hatch. Fortunately, the torpedo burned into a large spare parts and food storage compartment. Ear drums popping and gasping for their breath, crew members in adjacent spaces hung on to anything they could as the escaping air threatened to expel them into the vacuum of space. The automatic damage control system quickly isolated the compartments, allowing the ship to continue fighting.

"Two more torpedoes inbound, lasers locked on."

"Fire, fire," Miacon ordered.

One of the torpedoes was destroyed but the other one impacted the hull in the propulsion section of the ship.

"We've got about three minutes before the torpedo burns through and we lose our Ion Engines."

"Conning officer, prepare to ram."

"It's too soon to sacrifice the ship," he replied.

"With two Battle Cruisers damaged or lost and over a hundred Interceptors destroyed, the situation is becoming unmanageable."

"Miacon, we have detected two more Battle Cruisers."

"Mother-of-Lizards, Xentorcon has five Battle Cruisers. We must withdraw for the time being. This ship is lost. Order everyone into pressure suits. When I give the order, we'll abandon ship. Have the Interceptors disengage and prepare to pick up the crew."

The conning officer maneuvered the Shuttle to a heading equal to the relative bearing of one of Xentorcon's Cruisers and turned over ship control to the computer.

"Xentorcon, one of Miacon's Cruisers is heading straight for us."

"Bring all weapons to bare. They may blow up before they hit us."

"One minute to impact," Miacon's conning officer yelled.

"This is Miacon, cease engagement and transit to fourth planet from the sun. Interceptor squadrons 3 and 6 prepare to recover my crew, immediately."

"Xentorcon, Miacon is breaking off and heading away."

"I see them. All units cease fire."

"Abandon ship," Miacon ordered.

Miacon's crew began to abandon ship. Their fate was now in the hands of the Interceptor pilots. Miacon's crew spewed out of his ship like paratroopers in France on D-day. The Interceptors were ready and quickly picked them up.

Xentorcon maneuvered his ship sufficient to avoid a hard collision with Miacon's Cruiser. They passed hull to hull, scraping exterior structure off each ship but with no structural damage. It was like two speeding locomotives moving in opposite directions on tracks laid a little to close.

"All units, this is Xentorcon. The traitors have been routed. Believe they're heading to Mars for repairs and recovery. All units stand down, I say again, stand down and well done."

"Commander, I am returning to Earth, ETA one hour. Inform Ramacon and arrange for my arrival,"

"Sir, Ramacon perished in an accident. The ship he was being transported on blew up."

CHAPTER TWENTY-FOUR

The Invisible Liberator
Place: Portage La Prairie, Manitoba, Canada

Time: 1330 hours, August 11, 2050

JEREMIAH AND TACON HAD been huddled around their Ham Radio most of the day. Mary stood watch at the entrance to Jeremiah's quarters. The troopers would surely confiscate the radio if they discovered them listening to it. As long as they didn't transmit, they were relatively safe. The news that Miacon had retreated created a sense of despair. The news that the flu was disproportionately affecting the Rendinese was not received with sadness.

"We had better prepare ourselves for that long winter you talk about," Mary said.

"Miacon will figure something out."

"Well, I'm going to take an aspirin and lay down. I'm tired and feel congested." Mary said.

At the end of August, Portage medical reported they were seeing an unusually high number of Influenza cases and that several troopers had perished.

"It's a little early for full blown flu season, isn't it, Doc?"

"Normally, yes. The peak season is typically December through February, but at this latitude, this time of the year, the nights are cold and the flu virus likes cold air."

The transition from summer to fall happened in late September and, with no Indian Summer, winter rushed in with a vengeance in early November. One thing was clear, the Rendinese were becoming sick at an accelerating rate.

"Colonel, half of the troopers are sick with the flu. We're not doing much better. Seven deaths have occurred. We need to watch this carefully, we have no flu vaccine, so everyone is extra vulnerable, especially the Rendinese whose immune systems have never been exposed to many of our viruses."

"You suspect a Pandemic, Doc.?"

"It's possible. If it happens, it could be catastrophic for the Rendinese. The 1918 Epidemic in the US killed almost 700,000 people."

"The Flu might do what Miacon couldn't. Tonight, I'll check with a few BAS units around the country and see if they're observing the same thing. This may be a blessing in disguise," John said.

The next morning, Tacon, John, the medical officer and Jeremiah met for breakfast. Mary was sick with the flu and Jeremiah was not feeling well either. Attendance was minimal at breakfast. Only a couple of Troopers were present which is strange because they all love coffee.

"What did you find out last night," Tacon ask.

"Los Angeles, Chicago, and Miami reported similar rates of infection. The Rendinese are defiantly suffering. Most humans have been exposed or inoculated many times over the years, so we are not as vulnerable."

Back in his quarters, he was checking on Mary.

"Colonel, Fort Thompson is calling."

"Portage, this is Thompson, acknowledge," came over the radio again.

"Thompson, this is Portage, over."

"Portage, I need to speak with Colonel Astor."

"Speaking, go ahead."

"Colonel, what's happening. We're about to go crazy up here. I've had several desertions. I'm thinking about giving extended leave to my married soldiers and closing the Fort. We're accomplishing nothing up here."

"You'd be no better off down here, Major, we have a lot of sick people. How many soldiers are on the sick list?"

"None, why do you ask that?"

"Your far enough north and isolated, so it hasn't reached you yet, but we are in the middle of a flu epidemic and it's getting worse. I would consider staying where you are, but given the situation, with Xentorcon defeating Miacon, I'm not going to give you orders."

"Understand. I'll keep you informed."

"Bye the way, only call me on the mid watch."

"Understand, Thompson out."

The following week, things began to move in unexpected ways. BAS traffic was becoming increasingly belligerent. People sensed an opportunity, a vulnerability in their tormentors. The number of troopers being incapacitated or dying was still accelerating.

Humans were suffering too, but at one quarter the rate of the Rendinese. One night, Jeremiah received a call from Northern Command.

"Colonel Astor here."

"Colonel, this is General Walsh, I'm sure you're aware of the precarious position the aliens are in."

"Yes sir, we've been monitoring the circuits."

"We have divided North America up into engagement sectors. I'm placing you in command of all resistance operations in Manitoba. Organize your sector, including the BAS there, and prepare for further orders. You're now part of 'Operation Liberation'. D-Day is TBD. We're going to take back this planet or die trying. This is top secret, use cover stories or just lie if you have to, but discuss the operation with a minimum number of people"

"Understand General."

Place: The planet Mars

Time: 10:15 hours EST, November 20, 2050

Miacon had been working round the clock repairing his damaged ships. His space probes had been intercepting electronic signals from Earth since his engagement with Xentorcon. He knew Xentorcon's troops were pacifying Earth but were becoming increasingly sick.

Miacon had seen this before, both when bringing prisoners back to Xylanthia from other planets and when his own troops interacted with alien on their home planets. He assumed Xentorcon knew this also, which puzzled him. Miacon had his ship crews and troopers inoculated with a universal vaccine called Miroball. It was standard protocol and it amazed him that Xentorcon would fail to do so for a Reaper mission where his troopers would surely be exposed to alien disease.

"When Xentorcon's troops got so sick that they can no longer control the planet, I will strike." He thought.

Place: Xentorcon's Battle Cruiser

Time: 1420 hours EST, November 20, 2050

Xentorcon paced back and forth in his command center. His leaders had been giving him updates on the plague raging on the ground. Each report was worse than the last. This morning he was told that 65% of his troopers were so sick they could not report for duty and the death toll was up to 450.

He was thankful he stayed only one day on the ground after his defeat of Miacon, otherwise he might have brought the alien virus back to his ship. He was also angry with himself for not giving Microball injections to his crews and troopers before departure from Xylanthia. He assumed that medical had brought enough vaccine on board for use during the trip but there was a mix up. His risk to go ahead and pacify Earth anyhow was costing him dearly.

Place: Portage La Prairie, Manitoba, Canada

Time: 0830 hours, November 26, 2050

The Influenza pandemic was on steroids. 10% of the Rendinese positioned in and around Portage were dead, 70% were sick. BAS radio was reporting similar numbers all over North America. Jeremiah had organized his people, both military and civilian, into squads. They were told that in the event the Rendinese changed their tactics from pacification to genocide, we would rise up and fight, no matter what the odds were. Finally, the order came over the Ham Radio.

"Portage here, over."

"Colonel, D-day and time, November 30, 10:00 AM EST. No further communications will be made. Steal as many Rendinese weapons as possible and be on alert for reinforcements from Xentorcon's ships. Over."

"Acknowledged, out."

"Well Mary, as some one once said this could be the beginning of the end or liberation."

"It is ironic in a way," Mary lamented.

"How so?"

"That these powerful aliens are being defeated not by an army but by something invisible."

Jeremiah starred at Mary for a moment.

"What," she said.

Jeremiah dropped to one knee and took hold of her hand.

"Jeremiah, what are you doing?"

"Mary, you are the only woman I've ever loved. I don't want to depart this Earth having never been with the woman I love. Mary, would you honor me by being my wife?"

Mary dropped to her knees also and ran her fingers through his hair. She moved close to him and kissed him on the lips.

"I would be honored to be your wife."

Jeremiah got up and headed for the door.

"Where are you going?"
"To get the Chaplin. I don't want to wait."

That night Jeremiah and Mary were married with John and Tacon as witnesses. He spent the rest of the night taking Mary on a slow walk to the moon and back. In the morning, she teased him with some questions.

"Where did you learn to make love to a woman like you did to me last night?"
"Did you not like it?"
"You made me moan and yell so much I was embarrassed. You didn't learn that in a book."
"I know you don't believe me, but you are the first woman I've ever had intercourse with. My Dad told me about the rest of it."
"Oral expertise learned orally," she teased.
"Let's go to breakfast, I need some coffee."
"And we need to let our key leaders know the date and time."

CHAPTER TWENTY-FIVE

Operation Liberator
Place: Miacon's Battle Cruiser

Time: 0916 hours EST, November 27, 2050

MIACON HAD ARRANGED BEFORE leaving for Xylanthia, to use a low Megahertz frequency when communicating via space probe to Jeremiah and Tacon. Xentorcon would not normally monitor such low frequencies. He was encouraged but apprehensive about the message traffic from Earth. The news about D-day left him less than four days to prepare for battle and transit to Earth.

He ordered his ships to prepare for departure and nine hours later was on his way. He had two Battle Cruisers, ninety-seven Interceptors, and 700 troopers. His plan was to engage and distract Xentorcon enough to prevent him from reinforcing his troops on the ground prior to D-day.

Place: Portage La Prairie, Manitoba, Canada

Time: 0930 AM EST, November 30, 2050

John Rochester stood outside his quarters sipping tea like he used to do on the back porch of his Shenandoah, Virginia house. He wondered if it had been vandalized. He'd saved his last tea bag for a special moment and the moment was now. It was D-day with thirty minutes to go. Each second ticked off in his head like the steady heart beat in his chest.

At 0930 hours, soldiers and civilians slowly positioned themselves in predetermined places around the air field. The leaders knew their real purpose. The rest were told it was in preparation for defense against a possible Rendinese blood bath scheduled for 10:00 hours. The BAS had spread a story that the greatly weakened Trooper Corps planned to eliminate 50% of the humans to rebalance the power structure in North America.

At 10:00 hours, without sirens, bugles or whistles, 'Operation Liberator' began. The combined military and civilian force stepped out from behind trees, vehicles and doorways firing shot guns, assault rifles, hand guns and stolen Rendinese energy weapons.

All over North America, from Manitoba to Miami to Los Angeles, the scene was the same. Bullets and energy beams filled the air. Humans and Rendinese lost arms, legs, took head shots and dropped to the ground dead or mortally wounded. The death toll mounted on both sides.

This day however, there would be no surrender. Those who preferred slavery over death stayed hidden away in the woods, sewer systems, attics and abandoned mines. Anywhere that provided some measure of safety against the slaughter around them. Those who chose to fight were committed to victory or death.

In Portage La Prairie, Jeremiah ran around the back of a small building and found himself staring at a trooper standing ten feet away with his weapon pointed at him. They both looked at each other with fatalistic expressions, concluding they were both going to die. All of a sudden, the trooper took three rounds in the chest and dropped.

Jeremiah turned just in time to see John, who had saved him, be burned with a microwave weapon. The skin on his face turned pink, then blood red as the energy blast cooked his face and chest. He was dead before he started to fall. Jeremiah screamed in anger and emptied his assault rifle into the troopers who killed him.

Outside the mess facility, a BAS operative, using alcohol for courage, stepped out of a doorway and challenged a trooper to a gunfight. Like Gary Cooper in the movie High Noon, they faced each other. He had a whiskey bottle in his left hand and a revolver holstered on his right hip.

"Alright, you ugly son-of-a-bitch. I want your pony tail."

The trooper said something in Rendinese he didn't understand.

"If you took the shit out of your mouth, I could understand you. I'll assume you said come and get it."

The man drew his revolver and started firing. The alcohol didn't improve his aim. The third bullet nicked the trooper slightly in his upper left arm. The man stood with his gun now empty. The trooper slowly raised his weapon and blasted the man in the chest.

In the back of hanger #3, Jeremiah came to a conclusion. He pressed the talk button on his communicator and ordered his remaining fighters to disengage and retreat to the communication center. Last night they had quietly stacked sand bags around it. It was a good a place as any to put up a last defense. He knew the day was lost. He asks Mary to put the news out on the BAS frequency.

If Mary wasn't there, he might have fought on, but he was not going to allow her to suffer abuse from the Troopers or die a useless death. The day was lost because 9 troopers and 9 humans remained. Jeremiah knew that one-on-one, they were not going to win. He asked Tacon to offer a cease fire. He stepped out of the tent unarmed and yelled at a trooper, who was crouched down and throwing up. He was obviously sick with the flu.

"Trooper, we ask for a cease fire. We will stay here and take no further hostile action while you tend to your wounded."

The trooper used his communicator and a minute later yelled back that it was agreed. Chaos was replaced by calm and quiet.

Place: Xentorcon's Battle Cruiser

Time: 1046 hours EST, November 30, 2050

Xentorcon knew exactly what was happening on the ground. The flu and battle casualties had cost him 85% of his ground forces and his sensors told him Miacon was close. Xentorcon was faced with a dilemma. Focus his force on Miacon or reinforce his troopers on the ground? He couldn't do both at the same time.

"These humans continue to fight like bugs attacking a large animal. There are now too many of them and to few of us. They trade 100 lives for one trooper. At that exchange rate they will win in the end."

"We can end this with weapons of mass destruction."

"Yes, but we would kill many Rendinese and leave no one to work the planet. Remember our objective is to create Reaper colonies that support Xylanthia."

"Understand. We could deploy our remaining troopers and they could call for surgical strikes that would not kill troopers nor all of the humans."

"The process of landing troopers risk bringing the human sickness on board my Battle Cruisers. Miacon knows we are vulnerable and will strike us as soon as he is within range. I must deal with him first."

"Understand."

Place: Fort Thompson, Manitoba, Canada

Time: 1120 hours EST, November 30, 2050

Major Hunt was listening to the action reports on his Ham Radio. Not one Trooper had shown up at the fort or Baker Lake. Miami reported they'd driven the remaining three surviving Rendinese out of the city. Los Angeles had suffered over 2,000 casualties but were continuing the fight.

When Major Hunt heard the bad news from Portage, he made a decision. If Earth didn't cease this moment, if they didn't win, even out of the way places like Thompson would eventually be ravaged. He ordered his men to gas up all available vehicles. With 700 armed soldiers, BAS fighters and the remaining Proxima b pilgrims, the Fort Thompson convoyed headed south. Cargo was limited to medical supplies, ammo, food and extra gas.

It would take the better part of 12 hours to get to Portage. Like General Patton's race to relieve Bastogne in WW II, they drove without rest stops.

Place: Near Earth Space

Time: 1540 hours EST, November 30, 2050

Miacon's ships decelerated into the near-Earth space approximately one-million miles in altitude. Xentorcon was ready for him.

"Xentorcon, this is Miacon, reply."

"Xentorcon here, what are your intensions?"

"We could save a lot of Rendinese lives if you allow me to accept your surrender."

"I was thinking the same thing about you."

"Xentorcon, you are not in a good position. When I left Xylanthia, your dictatorship was in chaos. Now you are about to lose control of Earth. If we fight, you will be further weakened and your troops on the ground will perish, if not in battle, then from disease."

"Your lying about Xylanthia and your assessment of my tactical situation is flawed. When I dispense with you, I will reinforce my ground forces and destroy millions of humans. Victory will be mine.'

While Miacon was talking to Xentorcon, his Battle Cruisers were quietly launching interceptors. The Interceptors were told to keep his Battle Cruiser between them and Earth, hopefully minimizing their exposure to Xentorcon's sensors.

"Xentorcon, the number of Interceptors hovering around Miacon's Cruisers exceeds scout and patrol requirements. While you were talking, he was launching his attack force."

"That Ditch Snake."

Miacon nodded to his Operations officer to fire. Two hundred fusion powered hull burning torpedoes sped toward Xentorcon's ships. Xentorcon had to delay evasive maneuvers while he finished launching his Interceptors. Eight minutes later Miacon gave the order for his Interceptors to attack.

Dozens of torpedoes survived the brutal anti-torpedo fire from Miacon's ships. They slammed into Xentorcon's Cruiser's and began their burn. Like someone saying no, you can't come in, the super thick hulls resisted the rude and intrusive abuse from the torpedoes. The torpedoes would not be denied, many burned through the hulls.

Dozens of compartments were penetrated, causing rapid depressurization, death and expulsion into the cold vacuum of space. Computer controlled damage control systems quickly sealed off ruptured compartments preventing loss of the entire ship.

Miacon's Interceptors arrived in waves. Battle in the vacuum of space is brutal. Manual control of weapons was difficult due to the speed involved. Computer control fire control systems tracked and launched fire and forget ship-to-ship weapons as well as their onboard energy beams. If you were hit, it almost always meant death. Interceptors are flying bombs full of fuel, chemicals and ordnance.

Miacon was taking hits as well. On an even exchange rate, he knew he would lose. Xentorcon had more Cruisers and Interceptors. His objective was to delay reinforcement of the ground troops, not commit suicide. He ordered his Interceptors to withdraw.

Place: Portage La Prairie, Manitoba, Canada

Time: 0045 hours EST, December 1, 2050

Major Hunt could see the lights emanating from Portage. As he continued to approach, he was struck by how quiet it was. He ordered his drivers to maintain radio silence and turn off their lights. They would use Night Observation Googles the rest of the way.

Nine Rendinese and a half dozen seriously wounded troopers were gathered in Hanger #1. Several were sick. The leader was desperately trying to contact his commander for back up.

Major Hunt stopped his convoy a thousand yards from the Air Base and unloaded his soldiers. They would go on foot the rest of the way.

"Portage, this is Thompson," Hunt whispered into his radio."

"Thompson, this is portage, switch to channel seven. How are things up north?"

"Colonel, I am less than 800 yards from your location."

"Major, be advised that many here are sick."

"What is your tactical situation?"

"Many casualties. We've fought to a standstill and are currently engaged in a cease fire. Expect Rendinese reinforcements to arrive at any moment."

"They will not be expecting you to be reinforced. I intend to encircle the base and move in unison toward your position."

"The remaining Rendinese are in Hanger #1. That's the best place to converge. I'll meet you at the end of runway L6. We have absconded seven energy weapons which will even the odds a little."

"Very well, Thompson out."

Place: Near Earth Space

Time: 0200 hours EST, December 1, 2050

Miacon had little time to decide what to do. He knew Xentorcon would be reengaging. He was not going to run this time, no matter what. He needed a strategy.

"Miacon, they out number us three-to-one. We must depart the battle field."

"Not this time. There must be a way to even the odds."

"I wish I could get inside his cruisers with a few fusion bombs. The interior bulkheads can hold atmospheric pressure but not the over pressure from large ordnance."

"The only way into the interior is through the launch hangers."

Miacon looked at the large icons on his sensor screen.

"How do I make those ICONs go away?"

"There might be a way," a young officer blurted.

"Be silent," the Operations Officer said sternly."

"Let him speak," Miacon said.

"At the academy we studied many battles. In the history of our now collapsed universe, a great battle was fought between the technologically advanced Canopeons and the more primitive Alshainion empire. It was called the Pergon War.

The Canopeons were set to defeat the Alshainions. The Alshainion Commander ordered his fighters to ram the Canopeon ships and to detonate bombs near their propulsion nozzles. It cost the Alshainions many fighters, but the Canopeons were driven out of the battle space."

"Your suggesting we sacrifice the lives of our pilots, send them on a suicide mission," Miacon said.

"Miacon, the boy may have something. We don't need to sacrifice large numbers of pilots. If we had a dozen volunteers and targeted their launch bays? It could work."

Miacon ask for volunteers. Acceptance depended on a strict set of criteria. The pilots had to be single and have a personal grudge against Xentorcon's government. The dozen pilots chosen were either terminally ill, had family members abused or had a grudge against Xentorcon. One pilot's love interest had been brutally raped on Xylanthia by Xentorcon loyalists. In return, Miacon promised five years pay to whoever the pilots designated.

Interceptors were quickly loaded with two 500 Kilo-ton fusion bombs. The pilots assembled in the launch bay. Miacon spoke.

"Warriors of the empire. The mission you now embark on will determine the future of the Rendinese people. You will not be alone as you fly into destiny. Every loyal Rendinese and Rendinese ally will be in your cockpits. Your names will never be forgotten. May the spirits be with you."

The pilots scrambled into their Interceptors and prepared to launch. They waited for the green light above the hanger door to turn red, indicating the launch bay had completed depressurization. When the light turned red, the launch bay opened. Twelve Interceptors began their journey to infinity.

Three Interceptors were assigned to each of Xentorcon's four Battle Cruisers. They approached their targets with cockpit and running lights off, radio silence and squawking Xentorcon's fleet identification frequency.

"Commander, what are those interceptors up to. They should not be where they are."

"Unidentified ships, this is fleet command. Maintain your current distance and await orders," Xentorcon's Operations Officer ordered.

The Operations Officer suspected something was not right. Even in battle, Interceptors keep their running light on to aide in visual friend or foe determination. In addition, they were squawking an old code. Xentorcon's ships had changed codes after the initial engagement.

"Unidentified ships, this is Fleet Command. Acknowledge."

"Xentorcon, this is another Miacon trick. The unidentified ships are not responding."

"Air Control, twelve bogies incoming from sector three. Launch Interceptors. Weapons Control, deploy defensive guard."

The close in weapons system deployed an expanding cloud of death made up of thousands of golf ball size shrapnel. They could break cockpit crystal viewing ports, puncture holes in external fuel and chemical storage tanks and damage fly-by-wire control systems.

Xentorcon opened the launch bays on his Cruisers and began to deploy Interceptors. Miacon's Interceptors were now fifteen kilometers and closing. Two were destroyed by metal shrapnel impacting chemical tanks and wing mounted ordnance. Other's suffered nonlethal damage.

At nine kilometers they began a zig zag maneuver in hopes of avoiding energy beams. Nevertheless, three more Interceptors succumbed to continuous wave laser burns. At four kilometers, they could see the illumination from Xentorcon's launch bays.

RN-98 was the sole survivor of the approach to Xentorcon's cruiser. Her two wing mates had perished.

She aimed her ship at the launch bay. At 1 kilometer, the launch bay began to close. She promised her dead mate that she was coming home and set the fuse on her bomb for ten seconds. The launch bay door continued to close. She aimed her ship a low as she could without risking impact with the hull.

RN-98 met destiny the second it impacted the launch bay deck. The closure was so low, only the main fuselage of her ship made it through. The top of the Interceptor, including the cockpit, were cleaved off. Eight seconds later Xentorcon and his Battle cruiser became a rapidly expanding ball of gas, smoke, debris, and fire equivalent to a mini supernova.

Place: Portage La Prairie, Manitoba, Canada

Time: 0226 hours EST, December 1, 2050

Jeremiah and Major Hunt met at the end of runway L6 as agreed. The plan was to encircle and close in on Hanger #1. If the troopers would not drop their weapons, they would be killed. As they began to move out, the sky lit up like an eclipse in reverse. It was Xentorcon's cruiser exploding.

"Looks like Miacon has his hands full," Major Hunt said."
"Let's hope that explosion was Xentorcon's ship," Jeremiah replied.

Then a large object impacted hanger #3. It was the engine from an Interceptor. It came in like a comet and created a hyper-velocity impact crater twenty feet wide and fifteen feet deep.

"Damn, they're getting it on up there," a Sargent said.
"Looks like it, what I want to know is who is winning?"

With everyone in place outside of Hanger #1, Tacon used a bull horn to announce their presence and ask the troopers to surrender. They answered with the fury of a banzai charge. Red targeting beams created pointing vectors for microwave energy weapons.

Soldiers and BAS fighters responded with rifle and small arms fire and hand grenades. It sounded like the hanger was one big popcorn maker. Within minutes, dozens of soldiers and civilians went down. When it was over, thirty-two soldiers and civilians were dead or wounded. All but one of the troopers was dead. The ninth threw his weapon down and gave up.

"Sargent, lets clean this mess up. ID the BAS bodies so we can get them back to their families."

"Yes sir."

"Colonel, I suggest we check the BAS circuit. If we're losing big in other places, this is long from over."

"Agreed."

The BAS circuits were on fire with reports of capitulation by troopers all over North America. They were distracted by a sound they had heard before, the buzzing, popping and cracking of anti-gravity propulsors.

"That's the sound of an Interceptor landing, Tacon said.

"All units, take defensive positions," Jeremiah ordered over his communicator.

"Hold your fire," boomed out of the Interceptors external announcing system.

Jeremiah saw Miacon step out of the ship's exist portal.

"Don't fire, its Miacon," Tacon yelled.

"Colonel, Tacon, how's it going on the ground?"

"Heavy loss of life on both sides, but reports are good. Troopers are surrendering everywhere. I take it the explosions we saw were not your cruiser."

"No, but only due to the spirits and twelve brave pilots. I sent interceptors loaded with 500 kilo ton bombs into Xentorcon's launch bays. His cruiser and two others became part of the solar wind. Only one pilot survived."

"What happened to the rest of Xentorcon's fleet?"

"One cruiser and a number of Interceptors fled the solar system for deep space."

"Praise the lord. We still have the pandemic to deal with though. I hope your people have been inoculated."

"Yes, we have a universal vaccination. If Xentorcon's troopers had been vaccinated, we might have lost Earth."

"What do you want to do with the troopers on the ground?"

"Have your people transport them to a central location for triage and loyalty assessments."

"They have a large Internment camp near a town called Memphis," Jeremiah said.

"Send them there."

"A fitting end. Locking them up in their own prison," Mary said.

It took, several months for Miacon to accomplish mandatory maintenance and repairs, for the U.S. military and BAS to round up and transport troopers to Memphis, reestablish law and order and a functioning government.

Jeremiah's Missile sight construction battalion was d-commissioned. Major Hunt was promoted to Lieutenant Colonel and transferred to Quantico, Virginia. Jeremiah received word he was being promoted to General and ordered to Washington, D.C.

Miacon called Jeremiah to say he would be departing for Xylanthia in two days.

"Jeremiah, the time for me to return home is near. Earth will be fine now. Someday we will return, not as conquers but as allies."

Grace, Tacon, Abby and her children were listening.

"Jeremiah, ask him if he would transport some of us back to Proxima b."

"Miacon, please hold for a minute. Grace, are you sure that's what you want? Last time it didn't go very well."

"Yes, but I'm sure. That was John's dream. I want to take his body there so is grave will be near his loved ones."

"Miacon, any chance you could make a stop at Proxima b?"

"I could, some of my crew have said they would like to move there with their families. Where should I pick you up?"

"A place called Andrews Air Force Base. I'll get you the coordinates."

"Also, collect the supplies you will need to restart the colony."

"Will do, see you in a few days."

"Okay, you heard the conversation. We need everyone who's going to Proxima b at Andrews within 48 hours. I'll have some of my people stage the supplies for us."

"You said us. Jeremiah, we have been talking. We think you and Mary should remain on Earth. We need someone who knows the Rendinese and has the trust of the BAS civilians. Your voice will be a powerful influence for good moving forward."

"Tacon is right, we should stay," Mary said.

Two days later, Miacon's Interceptors were sitting on the tarmac at Andrews. After a few embraces, they loaded the supplies and everyone boarded the Interceptors. Once again, the buzzing, popping and cracking of anti-gravity propulsors filled the air. Miacon exited Earth's atmosphere leaving three distinct vapor trails that shear winds slowly turned from straight lines into the images of long snakes.

"Part of me wanted to go with them," Mary said.

"Maybe someday we'll visit," Jeremiah responded as he stared at the vapor trails.

"You know Abby and I are both pregnant. Our babies will be born four light years apart. Technically, they'll be aliens to each other."

"Technically, but they'll be fulfilling John's dream, and helping to secure the future of all intelligent life in the universe."

EPILOGUE

Ignoring history usually guarantees repeating it. Yet we do it all the time. There's never been a single example where socialism, communism or dictatorships have succeeded in the long run. Those economic and governing models either collapse or mutate into some form of representative democracy and capitalism. For some, it leads to a return to moneyless bartering on a distant planet.

The collapse of the Fourth Realm and Miacon's defeat of Xentorcon brought peace to the Orion-Cygnus Arm of the Milky Way Galaxy. Tacon and the Proxima b pilgrims built New America into a successful colony. By the turn of the 22nd century most had passed away.

Their legacy was a thriving integrated society of over 400 people. Tacon was the Mayor of Polaris, with Abby and their three children at his side, until he died. He is memorialized by a two-sided statue of him, one facing Earth, the other facing Xylanthia.

Some version of the events in this book will happen in the future. Earth's ability to deal with the reality that they are not alone will be the true measure of their worthiness to be part of the intergalactic community.

Lightning Source UK Ltd.
Milton Keynes UK
UKHW041839251119
354234UK00002B/31/P